INK BETWEEN US

-

SIMRAN MEHTA

BYTE & BIND

ISBN-13: 9781234567890
ISBN-10: 1477123456

Cover design by: BYTE & BIND
Library of Congress Control Number: 2018675309
Printed in the United States of America

There are letters meant for no one, and yet - somehow - they always find their way to the one who needs them most.

INK BETWEEN US

CONTENTS

TO YOU

CHAPTER : ONE

The bell above the door chimed softly as she stepped inside, the sound swallowed almost instantly by the silence of the bookstore. It was early—too early for customers—but she liked it that way. The stillness felt like a secret, something only she and the books shared.

She took a deep breath, inhaling the scent of old paper and ink, the quiet weight of forgotten stories pressing against the walls. She had always loved this place, with its creaky wooden floors and shelves that leaned ever so slightly, as if the books were whispering to one another. And now, it was more than just a place she loved—it was where she belonged.

She worked here.

It wasn't the kind of job most people would consider exciting, but she never wanted excitement. She wanted quiet, the kind that wrapped around her like a well-worn coat. She wanted the sound of pages turning, the way stories lingered in the air long after the books were closed. She wanted a space where time didn't rush forward but stretched, slowed, allowed her to breathe.

The store had no name. Or if it did, the sign outside had long since faded beyond recognition. It was one of those places that seemed to exist outside of time—unchanging, untouched by the rush of the world outside. People came and went, but the books remained, waiting.

Every morning, she unlocked the door, stepped inside, and let the world outside disappear for a little while. It was a small bookstore, tucked between two buildings as if hiding from the modern world. The windows let in just enough light to cast soft shadows on the wooden floor, and the shelves were packed tight, filled with books that had been loved and forgotten and loved again.

She moved through the narrow aisles, running her fingers along the spines of novels and poetry collections, memoirs and dusty old journals. There was something comforting about their presence, about knowing that every book held a piece of someone else's thoughts, their dreams, their heartbreaks—But today, something was different.

She felt it before she saw it—a strange pull, like a thread winding itself around her, tugging her toward the farthest shelf in the back. It was an unlit corner, where books were stacked haphazardly, some leaning, some toppling onto one another. The kind of place most customers ignored.

She hesitated, heart beating a little faster, but she didn't turn away. Instead, she reached out, drawn toward the disorganized pile. And then, without meaning to, she knocked a few books to the floor.

She sighed, bending down to gather them, but then her hands stilled.

There it was.

A single book, nestled beneath the others, its cover simple and unmarked except for the words embossed in faded gold lettering:

Ink between us.

She picked it up carefully, brushing her fingertips over the textured cover. It wasn't a title she recognized, and there was no author's name, no publishing mark. Just those three words.

It felt... old. Not in the way of the other books in the store, but in a different way. As if it had been waiting. As if it had been meant for her.

She opened it, and the pages whispered against her fingertips.

And then, she read.

The First Letter

Dear You,

I don't know who you are, not really. I don't know your name, your face, the way you smile when you find something funny or the way your voice might sound when you laugh. I don't know what keeps you up at night or what little things make your heart ache. But somehow, I feel like I know you—I wonder if this letter will ever reach you. I wonder if these words will ever make it into your hands, if your fingers will touch these pages like mine have, if your eyes will skim these lines and pause in the same places mine did while writing them.

I don't think I meant to write this—Not exactly. I just... needed somewhere to put my thoughts. Maybe you understand what that's like. That feeling, that quiet ache inside your chest when the world is moving too fast and you just need to get it all down before it slips through your fingers like sand. So, I did. I wrote. And I kept writing.

She exhaled, her fingers tightening around the book.

For a moment, she just stood there, staring at the page.

The letter was simple. Unassuming. But there was something about it—something that made her skin prickle, as if the words had reached out and wrapped themselves around her.

She flipped the page.

A Letter to No One (or Maybe Someone?)

I wonder who you are.

I wonder if you will ever write back.

She stopped.

Her breath caught in her throat.

This book—This wasn't just a collection of letters. It was something else entirely. It felt personal, as if the writer had reached across time and space and spoken directly to her.

And yet, it was impossible.

Wasn't it?

She glanced around the store, as if expecting someone to be watching. But she was alone. Just her and the book—Slowly, she closed it, running her fingers over the cover once more.

It felt warm.

Alive.

She should put it back. She should shake off the strange feeling curling in her stomach, the inexplicable sense that this book had been waiting for her.

But she didn't.

Instead, she held it tighter—her decision was made before she even realized it.

She was taking it with her.

And she was going to read every single letter.

CHAPTER : TWO

The bookstore felt different today. Or maybe it was her.

Anya stood behind the counter, the book resting on the worn wooden surface before her. Ink between us. The title felt heavier than it should, as if the words carried a meaning beyond their simplicity. It had consumed her thoughts ever since she found it hidden on the forgotten shelves—like it had been lying in wait, meant for her and her alone.

She traced her fingers over the cover again, the embossed letters rough beneath her touch. The book had made her feel—like it wasn't something merely to be read, but something meant to be experienced.

And yet, here she was again, unable to look away.

The store was quiet, the soft ticking of the clock above the door the only sound filling the space. It was early—too early for the usual customers who wandered in during lunch breaks or on their way home from work. Anya liked the quiet; it gave her time to think.

She exhaled slowly, flipping open the book to where she had left off, to read a line.

A Letter to No One (or Maybe Someone?)

I wonder who you are.

I wonder if you will ever write back to me.

She paused, staring at the words. There was something almost eerie about them, as if the writer had known she would find this book one day. But that was impossible. This was a book—pages and ink and old paper. And yet...

Anya shook her head, closing the book and pressing her fingers against her temples. She was overthinking. It was a coincidence, nothing more. Still, the feeling lingered.

She glanced around the store, as if expecting to find some kind of answer hidden between the shelves. Sunlight streamed through the large front window, dust motes floating lazily in its golden glow. Everything looked normal. Everything was normal.

And yet, the book sat there, waiting.

Anya sighed, running a hand through her hair before looking back down at it. Maybe she just needed to make a decision. She had spent too much time debating, too much time hesitating.

She picked up the book again and held it in her hands, feeling its weight.

It wasn't like she had never bought a book before—she worked in a bookstore, for God's sake. But this wasn't about buying a book; it was about this book.

Something inside her whispered that once she made the decision, there would be no going back.

But she didn't want to go back.

Anya reached under the counter, pulling out her wallet. She hesitated for only a second before sliding out a few bills and placing them in the register. The old machine dinged softly as she rang up the purchase, the finality of the action settling deep in her bones.

She owned it now.

She picked up the book again, this time with a strange sense of reverence. It was hers. Whatever this was—whatever these letters would reveal—it belonged to her now.

Anya turned it over in her hands once more before slipping it into her bag.

She didn't know what she would find in its pages. But one thing was certain.

She was going to find out.

CHAPTER : THREE

The First Letter

Anya reached her apartment just as the sun dipped below the horizon, casting the city in hues of gold and purple. The journey home had been uneventful—the usual bus ride filled with the murmurs of tired passengers, the rhythmic hum of the engine lulling her into a quiet daze. She unlocked her door, stepped inside, and let out a long breath, the weight of the day settling over her shoulders like an old, familiar coat.

Tossing her keys onto the small wooden table by the door, she kicked off her shoes and set her bag down. The apartment was quiet, save for the distant hum of traffic outside. It was a small space, but cozy. The soft glow of a bedside lamp bathed the room in golden light, casting long shadows on the walls.

She moved through the motions of her routine almost absentmindedly—putting a kettle on for tea, changing into comfortable clothes, tying her hair up into a messy bun. The day had been uneventful. A handful of customers came and went, browsing the aisles, flipping through books they probably wouldn't buy. Some people had asked for recommendations, and she had done what she always did—offered suggestions based on what she thought they might like, only to be met with noncommittal nods before they placed the books back where they found them.

But through it all, one thing had remained constant.

That book.

Even as she closed the door behind her, turned the lock, and made her way to the small, secondhand couch by the window, she felt its presence in her bag. It was strange, really. It wasn't as though she hadn't found interesting books before—after all, she worked in a bookstore. She was surrounded by words every day, by stories waiting to be read.

And yet, this book—Ink between us—felt different.

She settled onto the couch, tucking her legs beneath her, and pulled the book from her bag. The cover felt slightly rough under her fingers, as if it had been handled often, yet the pages were crisp and untouched, waiting to be read.

Anya sipped her tea, set the cup down on the small wooden table beside her, and ran her fingertips along the spine of the book.

For a moment, she hesitated.

She had no idea what was inside, and yet, something in her whispered that once she started, there would be no turning back.

She flipped it open.

The pages had no traditional title, no table of contents, no introduction. Just a single phrase
To You.

Anya's brow furrowed slightly. She glanced toward her

window, as if expecting to see some unseen force watching her, before shaking her head. Silly. It was just a book. Just an ordinary book.

And yet, as she let her eyes settle on the words, the world outside seemed to fade away.

Dear You,

I don't know who you are, not really. I don't know your name, your face, the way you smile when you find something funny or the way your voice might sound when you laugh. I don't know what keeps you up at night or what little things make your heart ache. But somehow, I feel like I know you.

I wonder if this letter will ever reach you. I wonder if these words will ever make it into your hands, if your fingers will touch these pages like mine have, if your eyes will skim these lines and pause in the same places mine did while writing them.

I don't think I meant to write this. Not exactly. I just... needed somewhere to put my thoughts. Maybe you understand what that's like, that feeling, that quiet ache inside your chest when the world is moving too fast and you just need to get it all down before it slips through your fingers like sand. So, I did. I wrote. And I kept writing.

That's how I found myself here, writing to someone I don't even know. Writing to you.

I don't know if you believe in fate. I never used to. But lately, I find myself wondering if maybe, just maybe, there is something at work beyond what we can see. Because what are the odds that you'd pick up this book, that you'd turn these pages and read my words, my thoughts? What are the odds that, even though we've never met, you'd be sitting somewhere right now, hearing my voice in your head as you read this?

It's strange, isn't it?

Do you believe that things happen for a reason, that people come into our lives at just the right moment? Or do you think everything is random—that we're all just drifting through this life, colliding with each other by chance?

I don't know which I believe.

Maybe you don't either.

But either way, I'm glad you're here.

It means you found me. It means, in some way, I found you too.

And maybe... maybe that means something.

I should go. But if you want to read more, turn the page.

Soren

Anya let the book fall shut in her lap, her hands motionless over the cover.

Soren. So that was his name. She stared at the book, the weight of it pressing against her legs as if daring her to process what she had just read. A simple, almost accidental letter—one meant for no one, and yet, somehow, meant for her.

She traced the name on the cover with her fingertip, heart thudding a little faster than it should.

She didn't believe in fate.

Or at least, she hadn't before.

But now, she wasn't so sure.

And she knew, without a doubt, she would turn the page.

CHAPTER : FOUR

The Second Letter

Dear You,

I wonder—do you ever think about all the people you'll never meet?

I don't mean the ones who live on the other side of the world or the ones whose lives are separated from yours by decades, even centuries. I mean the ones who might have walked past you on the street today, the ones who sat across from you on the bus or brushed shoulders with you in a crowded café.

Have you ever made eye contact with a stranger and felt... something? That quick jolt of familiarity, that fleeting sense of recognition, as if for the briefest second you knew them and they knew you? And then, just as quickly, the moment passed, and they were gone, and you were left wondering if they even noticed you at all?

I think about that sometimes.

I think about how many people I might have walked past in a crowded bookstore—people who could have been friends if only I had stopped to say hello. I wonder how many stories I've missed out on, how many "almost" connections have slipped through my fingers. I think about how, in another life, you and I could have been something more than just a writer and a reader. But even now, even in this quiet and lonesome way, I'm glad we found each other.

Because if you're reading this, that means my words found their way to you. And maybe that's enough.

Maybe words are all we need to bridge the spaces between us.

I've always been fascinated by words—the way they can create worlds, the way they can bring comfort when everything else feels like too much. I've always believed words have power—real power—not the kind you see in fairy tales, but the kind that makes you feel seen. I don't know what you're going through, but I know you're here, and that means something.

Maybe you picked up this book out of curiosity. Maybe

you were drawn to it without knowing why. Maybe you were looking for something, some sort of answer you don't even know you need yet.

Or maybe you're like me, and sometimes you just need a place to put your thoughts.

So, tell me, who are you? I wish I could know. I wish I could hear your voice as you whisper my words in your mind, could see the way your eyes move across these lines, taking in every letter. Are you curled up in bed? Are you reading this on a train, lost in your own world? Are you at a café, the scent of coffee mixing with the soft, ink-stained pages of this book?

Wherever you are, whoever you are—I hope you stay a little longer.

Because I have so much more to say.

Until next time,

Soren

Anya stared at the words on the page, her fingers gripping the edges of the book just a little tighter.

Soren's words had a way of settling into her bones, making her feel as though he wasn't just writing to no one—he was writing to her. It was absurd, of course. He had no idea who she was, no way of knowing she would ever pick up this book. And yet, there was something about the way he phrased things, the way he reached across time and space to ask questions she had never dared to say out loud, that made her feel seen in a way she couldn't quite explain.

Did she ever think about all the people she would never meet?

Anya exhaled slowly, sinking back into the cushions as she thought about her routine; she had spent years surrounded by books, slipping in and out of stories, living a thousand lives that weren't hers. But never—not once—had she thought about all the people she might have met if only she had looked up at the right moment. She thought about the strangers she had passed on her way to work, the nameless faces in cafés, the fleeting glances exchanged in crowded trains. Had any of them ever wondered about her, the way Soren wondered about the reader of his letters? Has she ever been an "almost" in someone else's story?

The thought unsettled her.

Maybe it was just the way he wrote. There was something about Soren's words that felt too intimate, too familiar, like he wasn't just speaking to a nameless, faceless stranger but to her—Anya—specifically.

She traced her fingertips over his signature at the end of the letter. Soren. Whoever he was, he wrote like he believed words could change things—like they could reach someone, even when the person writing them had no idea who would ever read them.

Anya glanced up from the book, her gaze settling on the large front window. Outside, the world carried on as usual—people walking by, lost in their own lives, unaware of the stories they might be passing.

And suddenly, she couldn't shake the thought:

What if she had walked past Soren once? What if, without even realizing it, she had been an "almost" in his life, too?

The idea lingered, wrapping itself around her like a quiet whisper.
For now, she just needed a moment to sit with the words.

CHAPTER : FIVE

The Third Letter

Anya sat curled up on her bed, the book resting on her lap, its pages still warm from where her fingers had lingered. She had promised herself she would wait until morning —let the words settle—but she couldn't. The quiet of her apartment only made Soren's voice in her mind louder, his words pulling at something deep inside her. With a sigh, she reached for the book again, flipping it open with a quiet urgency. Her pulse quickened as her eyes found the next letter. It felt foolish, this impatience, but she couldn't help it. She needed to keep reading.

Dear You,

Have you ever had one of those moments that made you stop and wonder if everything really is just random? Or if, maybe—just maybe—there's something more, some invisible thread pulling things into place, guiding them toward where they're meant to be?

I used to believe in coincidences. I used to think life was just a series of accidents, that things happened because they happened, without meaning or purpose. But then, small things started to make me question that belief.

Like the time I was thinking about an old friend I hadn't spoken to in years, and just as I reached for my phone to search for their number, their name appeared on my screen, calling me as if they had felt the same pull. Or the time I took a different route home for no reason at all only to run into someone I had been hoping to see.

And now—this.

You, holding this book. Reading these words.

What are the chances?

What are the chances that I would sit down one day and write these letters, never knowing if anyone would read them, never knowing who they would be for? And what are the chances that, out of all the books on all the shelves in all the places you could have been, you found this one?

I suppose a logical person would say it's nothing special, that books are bought, borrowed, or stumbled upon every day, that I wrote these words and eventu-

ally someone was bound to read them.

But I'm not sure I believe that.

Not entirely.

Because when I think about you—yes, you—I can't shake the feeling that maybe this wasn't just a chance.

Maybe these letters were always meant to reach you. Maybe this book has been waiting for you just as much as you've been waiting for it. Maybe, in some way I can't explain, I was always writing to you.

Does that sound strange?

I know we don't know each other. Not really. But isn't that the beauty of this, that two strangers, separated by time and distance, can still find each other in the spaces between ink and paper—that words written in solitude can one day land in the hands of the one person who was always meant to read them?

Tell me—do you believe in coincidences?

Or do you think everything happens for a reason?

I used to think the universe was indifferent, that it didn't care where we ended up or who we became. But now, I wonder if it nudges us—just a little—toward the things we need to find.

I wonder if it led you here.

Maybe this is nothing, just another book, just another moment in your day. Maybe you'll close this soon and never think of it again. But maybe—just maybe—you'll stay. And if you do, if you turn to the next page, I hope you'll consider the possibility that we were always meant to meet—

In this quiet, wordless way.

Until next time,

Soren

Anya turned the page.

CHAPTER : SIX

The Fourth Letter

Dear You,

I don't know your name. I don't know where you are as you read this. I don't know the colour of your eyes or the way your voice sounds when you say your own name aloud. But still, I feel like I know you.

Not in the way the world defines knowing—not through introductions, shared conversations, or familiar glances across a crowded room. I don't know the shape of your days or the weight of the memories you carry. But somehow, through these words, through this fragile, invisible thread that ties us together, I know something about you.

I know that you are the kind of person who notices the little things.

You pay attention in ways most people don't. Maybe you notice the way the sunlight filters through the trees, casting golden patterns on the sidewalk. Maybe you stop to listen to the sound of rain against the window—hearing it, feeling it—like a song only you understand. Maybe you watch people when they aren't looking, observing the way their hands move when they talk or the way their eyes dim just a little when they say, "I'm fine," but mean something else entirely.

I know you care more than you let on.

You pretend that things don't affect you as deeply as they do, but the truth is, they stay with you. You carry them—words spoken and unspoken, moments fleeting but unforgettable. You remember the things others forget: the way someone once looked at you like you were their whole world, or the way another walked away as if you were nothing. You replay conversations in your mind long after they've ended, thinking about what you could have said, what you should have said, what you wish you had the courage to say.

I know you feel things intensely, even if you don't always show it.

You can hear a song and feel it in your bones. A single line in a book can haunt you for days. You fall in love with places, with words, with ideas—sometimes more than you do with people. Maybe that's why you're here, reading this letter. Because you understand what it's like to feel connected to something—or someone—you've never met.

I know that you long for something you can't quite name.

You lie awake at night, staring at the ceiling, feeling like there's something missing, something just out of reach. Maybe it's a person, a place, a version of yourself you haven't met yet. Maybe it's love, or adventure, or simply the feeling of being truly understood. Whatever it is, I know it's there—a quiet ache, a whisper of longing that never really goes away.

I know you've been hurt before

Not just in the obvious ways, but in the silent, unseen ones. Maybe someone left when you thought they never would. Maybe you loved someone who couldn't love you back. Maybe you gave too much of yourself to someone who only wanted pieces of you. Or maybe it wasn't a person at all—maybe life itself let you down in ways you never expected.

But I also know that despite it all, you're still here.

You still hope, even if you don't always admit it. You still dream, even when the world tells you it's foolish. You still search for something—connection, meaning, a sign that you're not alone in all of this. And if you're reading this, if you've made it this far, maybe this is your sign.

Maybe this is proof that even in the vastness of this world, even in all its chaos and unpredictability, there are still moments of quiet magic—like this one. A letter from someone you've never met, speaking to you as if they know you. And in some strange, unexplainable way, maybe I do.

Because you are the kind of person who picks up a book not just to read, but to feel.

You are the kind of person who listens to the spaces between words.

You are the kind of person who finds meaning in things others overlook.

And that tells me more about you than you realize.

So maybe I don't know your name. Maybe I don't know

where you are as you read this. But I know you're here. And that's enough for now.

Until next time,

Soren

Anya let out a slow breath, her fingers tightening around the edges of the book as she reread the last few lines.

How could someone who didn't even know her put into words everything she had never been able to explain about herself? It was unsettling—like Soren had reached into her mind, plucked out her unspoken thoughts, and laid them bare on the page.

She traced the inked letters with her fingertip, feeling a strange sense of recognition, as if this letter had been meant for her all along.

A quiet shiver ran through her.

She wasn't sure what to feel.

Anya exhaled softly, her fingers trembling slightly. Unable to resist, she turned the page, eager to read the next letter.

CHAPTER : SEVEN

The Fifth Letter

Dear You,

I thought about calling you by a different name.

Something unique, something just ours—something that could bridge the space between us. After all, words create closeness, don't they? A name is an anchor, a tether, a way to make someone real even when they're far away. If I gave you a name, perhaps you would feel more tangible, less like a fleeting thought in the night and more like someone I could reach across the distance and touch.

But nothing felt right.

I considered the classics—those names that roll off the tongue like poetry, soft and familiar. I considered names that carried weight, names with history, names that whispered stories even in their silence. But none of them belonged to you. None of them captured what I wanted to say.

And then it hit me.

You.

A simple word. A single syllable. But somehow, it felt like everything.

You.

It holds the weight of a thousand possibilities. It feels personal yet universal. It's a word that can mean anyone, but when I write it, I mean only you.

I like the way it sounds in my mind when I think of you—how easily it settles into my sentences, how naturally it shapes itself around my thoughts. There's no hesitation in it. No pretense. It simply is.

It's strange, isn't it? How one word can hold so much meaning, how it can make someone feel seen even when they remain unseen.

Because 'you' is not just a name—it's a feeling.

It's the pause before someone says something important. It's the lingering weight of a gaze held a second too long. It's the silence between words that speaks louder than anything else.

'You' is the person in the room who makes your heart beat differently. It's the memory that stays even when everything else fades. It's the thought that lingers at the edge of sleep, the whisper in the back of your mind when you least expect it.

It feels right, doesn't it?

I like that I can write to you without barriers—that I don't need to define you to speak to you. Maybe that's why this feels different from everything else. Because this isn't a letter addressed to just anyone; it's addressed to you.

Whoever you are. Wherever you are.

And yet, I wonder... Do you think of me the same way?

When you turn these pages, do you picture a face? Do you imagine a voice behind these words? Or am I just ink on a page, a ghost whispering through paper and time?

If I were to give myself a name, would it change things?

Would I become more real to you?

Or would it break the spell?

Because maybe that's the magic of this—this space between knowing and not knowing, between recognition and mystery. Maybe the fact that you don't know me, and I don't know you, is what makes this special. Maybe if we knew each other too well, this would turn into something ordinary, something predictable. And I don't want that.

I want this to remain as it is—limitless.

So I won't name you.

For now, we will be You and I.

And maybe, just maybe, that's all we ever need to be.

Until next time,

Soren

Anya traced her fingers over the word You, letting it linger on her lips in a whisper only she could hear. It was such a simple name, yet it felt strangely intimate, as if it had been chosen just for her—not a label, not an identity to wear, but a feeling: fluid, personal, infinite. She liked that.

It made her wonder—was Soren real, or just a voice born from ink and longing?

Either way, she found herself sinking deeper into the letters, as if You had always been hers to claim.

And so, she kept reading.

CHAPTER : EIGHT

The Sixth Letter

Dear You,

I have a secret.

It's not the kind of secret that shakes the world—not the kind that makes headlines or carries weight in whispered conversations behind closed doors. No, it's much simpler than that.

But sometimes, the simplest secrets are the heaviest ones.

I am lonely.

It feels strange to write that down, as if admitting it makes it more real, as if, by giving it shape through words, I can no longer hide from it.

But maybe that's the point.

I don't know when loneliness became a part of me. I don't know if it crept in slowly, settling into my bones over time, or if it arrived suddenly—like a wave crashing against the shore, swallowing everything in its path.

I just know that it's here.

It lingers in the silence of my room, in the spaces between conversations. It follows me through crowded streets, pressing against my skin like an invisible weight. It sits beside me at night, a quiet presence that never speaks but never leaves.

And the strangest part?

No one notices.

No one looks at me and sees it. No one asks if I'm okay. Maybe because I've gotten good at hiding it. Maybe because I've learned how to smile in all the right places, how to laugh when expected, how to nod and agree and carry on as if everything is fine.

Or maybe because everyone else is just as lonely as I am.

Maybe we're all pretending.

I wonder if you know this feeling, too.

If you've ever sat in a room full of people and felt like you were miles away from them. If you've ever laughed at a joke but felt no warmth in it. If you've ever wished someone would ask how you're really doing—not out of politeness, not as a formality, but because they truly wanted to know.

Because even though I don't know you—even though I have no idea who you are, where you are, or what kind of life you live—I want to believe that someone is listening.

That someone is out there, reading this, understanding it.

That I'm not just speaking into the void.

Is that selfish?

Is it selfish to want to be heard—to want someone, anyone, to look at these words and think, I see you?

I think we all want that, in some way. To be seen. To be understood.

But we don't always say it out loud, do we?

Instead, we keep it inside. We carry it like a secret, tucked away in the corners of our hearts, too afraid to let it slip—because admitting it means acknowledging the ache. And acknowledging the ache means confronting the fact that we don't know how to fix it.

I don't know how to fix it.

I don't know if writing these letters will change anything. I don't know if putting my thoughts into words will make the loneliness feel any less suffocating. But I do know this:

For the first time in a long time, I don't feel invisible.

Because right now, at this moment, I am writing to you. And even though I don't know if you're truly there—

even though I don't know if these words will ever reach anyone at all—I choose to believe that they will.

That you will read them. That you will hear me. That you will understand.

And somehow, that's enough.

So, if I tell you a secret, will you keep it?

Will you hold these words in your heart, even for just a little while?

Will you remember that somewhere, someone once wrote this letter—not because they had to, but because they needed to? Because they hoped, more than anything, that someone like you would find it?

Until next time,

Soren

Anya let out a slow breath, her fingers curling around the edges of the page as if holding it tighter would anchor her to the moment. Loneliness—such a simple word, yet so heavy when laid bare like this.

She wasn't sure what unsettled her more: the raw honesty of Soren's confession or the way it mirrored something deep within her.

She had always thought of loneliness as something quiet, something nameless that crept into the spaces between her days. But now, reading this, she realized—maybe she had been carrying the same secret all along.

And for the first time, she wasn't sure if she was reading a letter meant for her or if she had stumbled upon a letter she could have written herself.

CHAPTER : NINE

The book lay open in Anya's lap, its pages slightly curved from how tightly she had been holding them. The quiet hum of the night surrounded her, broken only by the occasional creak of the house settling. She had stopped reading a while ago, her gaze fixed on the words but her mind elsewhere.

She wasn't sure how long she had been staring at the same page, lost in thought.

Soren's words lingered in her mind, refusing to be forgotten.

"I am lonely."

She closed her eyes.

It was such a simple sentence, yet it carried so much weight. It wasn't poetic or exaggerated—just the raw, unembellished truth. And somehow, that truth had wrapped itself around her, making her feel exposed in a way she hadn't expected.

Wasn't she just fine?

She had a routine, a stable job, and a quiet life. She wasn't miserable. And yet, the way Soren had described loneliness—as something that could exist even in a room full of people, something that sat beside you in the quiet moments—felt too familiar.

Maybe that's why she had stopped reading.

Not because she wanted to, but because she needed to.

Because reading more meant confronting something she wasn't sure she was ready to face.

She ran her fingers over the book's worn pages, hesitating. She could close it now, call it a night, pretend that these letters were just words on a page and not something reaching into the deepest corners of her thoughts. She could, but she wouldn't.

Because even though she had paused, the words wouldn't let her go.

So she started reading it back.

Minutes passed. Maybe Hours.

The clock on the wall ticked steadily, the glow of her bedside lamp casting long shadows across the room, but Anya was only vaguely aware of her surroundings. The world outside the book barely existed anymore.

Soren's letters pulled her in, unraveling piece by piece, making her forget that she had planned to stop. She kept telling herself, "Just one more," but every time she reached the end of a letter, she couldn't bring herself to close the book.

Because each letter felt like a conversation left unfinished —like something waiting to be understood.
She shifted, hugging her knees to her chest as she read on.

"If I tell you a secret, will you keep it?"

Anya swallowed.

She already had.

She had kept every word, tucked them away in the corners of her mind, carrying them even when she wasn't reading.

She had started this book out of curiosity. But now?

Now, it felt like something more.

And she wasn't sure she could walk away.

CHAPTER : TEN

The Seventh Letter

Dear You,

I wonder how closely you're paying attention—not just to the words, but to what's hidden beneath them. Not just to what I say, but to what I don't.

There is an art to reading between the lines, you know. Some people skim through words, taking them at face value, never pausing to wonder if there's something more. Others—people like you, I think—understand that words are often just the surface of something deeper; that there are meanings tucked away between sentences, emotions folded carefully into the spaces where ink doesn't reach.

So, tell me, You.

Have you been paying attention?

If you have, then maybe you already know that these letters aren't just letters. Maybe you've already sensed that this isn't just about writing or about filling blank pages with idle thoughts.

Maybe you've already felt it:

the weight of unspoken things, the quiet hesitations, the way I sometimes dance around the truth instead of facing it head-on.

Maybe you've noticed that I ask more questions than I answer.

Maybe you've seen the way I leave certain things unsaid.

Or maybe you haven't.

Maybe you're just reading this the way one reads any other letter, absorbing the words but not the silences. Maybe you're letting my sentences wash over you without wondering about the spaces between them.

I wouldn't blame you.

It's easier that way, isn't it?

It's easier to take things as they are, to accept the words on the page without questioning what's hiding underneath. It's easier not to look too closely, not to search too deeply. Because once you start seeing the spaces between the words, you start realizing how much they carry—how much I carry.

And the truth is, You—I carry a lot.

I've always been good at hiding things in plain sight—at slipping truths into sentences where no one thinks to look, at burying emotions between commas and pauses, tucking them away in metaphors and half-finished thoughts.

It's a habit, I suppose. A kind of self-preservation.

Because if no one notices what's beneath the words, then they don't ask questions. And if they don't ask questions, then I don't have to find answers.

But you're different.

I don't know how I know that. Maybe it's just a feeling. Maybe it's wishful thinking. Maybe it's the way I imagine you reading these letters—not just with your eyes, but with something deeper.

I think you see more than most.

I think you read between the lines.

And that terrifies me.

Because if you do—if you really, truly do—then you must know by now that there are things I'm not saying, that there are emotions pressing against the edges of my sentences, too big to be contained, too fragile to be fully spoken.

You must know that these letters, for all their words, are still incomplete.

There are things I want to say but can't, feelings I have yet to name, fears I haven't admitted, longings I barely understand myself.

I wonder if you see them.

I wonder if you understand.

And if you do—if you've been reading between the lines all this time—then I have another question for you.

Do you ever do the same?

Do you ever find yourself holding things back, hesitating at the edge of a truth you're not sure how to say? Do you ever wonder if someone will notice the silences in your own words—if they'll sense the emotions hidden beneath your carefully chosen phrases?

Do you ever wish someone would read between your lines the way I hope you're reading between mine?

Because I would.

If you ever wrote back—if you ever let me see even a glimpse of who you are—I would read every word carefully. I would look for the spaces between your sentences, the pauses that

mean more than they should. I would listen to what you don't say as much as to what you do.

And I would understand.

Or, at least, I would try.

Maybe that's why I keep writing.

Because some part of me hopes that you see what I can't say, that you recognize it, that you won't turn away from it—from me.

So, if you're still here—if you're still reading—let me ask you one last thing.

Have you found the unspoken words yet?

And if you have...

What do they tell you?

Until next time,

Soren

CHAPTER : ELEVEN

The Eighth Letter

Dear You,

I've been thinking—about these letters, about the way I write them, about the way you—wherever you are—might be reading them.

I used to think of them as monologues, just me spilling my thoughts onto paper, sending them into the void without expecting anything in return—a one-sided conversation, a voice speaking into the dark.

But that's not how it feels anymore.

Somewhere along the way, I stopped writing like I was talking to myself. Somewhere along the way, I started writing to you. Really to you.

And isn't that what a conversation is?

I ask questions, even though I know I won't get answers. I imagine your reactions, your expressions, the way your fingers might linger over certain words. I wonder if you're laughing at my silly thoughts, frowning at my confessions, pausing when something I say resonates with you.

Maybe that's enough.

Maybe words don't need a voice speaking them aloud to be heard. Maybe letters don't need replies to be conversations.

Maybe this—this thing we have, whatever it is—is real in its own way.

I wonder if you talk back to me sometimes—if you answer my questions in your head, if you whisper thoughts to the pages even though you know I can't hear them. Maybe you roll your eyes when I get too philosophical. Maybe you nod when something makes sense. Maybe you write me back in your mind, even if the words never leave your lips.

It's funny, isn't it? How words can build connections even when only one of us is speaking—how a letter can feel like a dialogue, even when I'll never know what you'd say in return.

But maybe I don't need to know.

Maybe it's enough that you're here, that you're reading, that for a moment our thoughts exist in the same space, even if we'll never truly meet.

Because that's what a conversation is, isn't it? Not just words exchanged, but understanding shared.

And I like to think you understand.

I like to think that when you read my words, you don't just skim them. You feel them—you let them settle inside you the way they settled inside me before I wrote them down. I like to think that even though I'm just some anonymous voice on a page, you're listening.

Really listening.

Because I am, too—listening to the silence between my

own words, the things I don't say, the emotions that slip between the lines. Listening to the possibility that somewhere you are reading this and feeling the same way—

that you hear me.

That this is a conversation, even if it only goes one way.

And if it is—if these letters truly are a conversation—then let me ask you something.

Are you listening to yourself, too?

Because I wonder, sometimes, if you do the same thing I do—if you leave things unsaid, if you hold thoughts inside because you're not sure anyone would understand them, if you have conversations in your mind that never find their way into the world. Maybe you're like me.

Maybe you, too, have words locked inside that you wish someone would hear.

If that's the case, then let me tell you this:

I am listening.

Even if I can't hear you, even if I don't know your voice or your name, even if these letters are the only thing connecting us—

I am listening.

To the possibility of you.

To the silence between my words, where your answers might exist.

And maybe—just maybe—that's enough to turn these letters into something real.

Until next time,

Soren

Anya sat still, the letter resting lightly between her fingers, but she felt its weight pressing down on her. The quiet hum of the night wrapped around her, but inside, her thoughts were loud—louder than they had been in a long time.

She had been reading this book for hours now, but something about this letter felt different. It was like Soren wasn't just writing to fill the space in his own mind—he was reaching out. And
Into her.

"Are you listening to yourself, too?"

The question settled in her chest, uncomfortably close to something she had never dared to confront.

Was she?

She had spent so much time listening to others—at work, at home, in conversations that felt more like transactions than connections. She had mastered the art of nodding at the right moments, of offering polite smiles, of responding with the right words even when she didn't feel them.

But when was the last time she had truly listened to herself?

The thought unnerved her.

She exhaled, running her fingers through her hair, suddenly feeling restless.

Soren was a stranger—a faceless, nameless writer who existed only in ink and paper. And yet he had managed to make her feel seen in a way no one else had.

She wanted to argue with the letter, to insist that this wasn't a conversation, that he didn't know her. But the truth was, she had been talking back to him all along, hadn't she? In her mind, in the pauses between sentences, in the moments she caught herself nodding along to his words.

Maybe you write me back in your mind, even if the words never leave your lips.

Anya swallowed hard.

How had he known?

She placed the book down on the table, rubbing her palms against her jeans. She needed to take a break—to shake off this strange, unsettling feeling curling inside her.

But she didn't move.

Because even as she told herself she should stop, that she needed sleep, she knew she wouldn't close the book.

Not yet.

Because at this moment, more than anything, she wanted to keep listening.

CHAPTER : TWELVE

The Ninth Letter

Dear You,

A Memory I Want to Share With You

There's a place I used to go when I was younger—a small hill just outside the town where I grew up. It wasn't anything particularly special, just a gentle slope covered in tall grass, a few scattered trees swaying in the wind, and a view that stretched far beyond what my young mind could comprehend.

I found it by accident one summer when I was a child. I don't even remember why I was wondering that day, only that I had been following a narrow dirt path, kicking stones and humming to myself. It led me through a field of wildflowers, golden in the late-afternoon light, and then, suddenly—as if I'd walked through an invisible door—the trees opened up and revealed the hill.

It wasn't the highest point in town, but from up there I could see everything: the rooftops of houses like tiny squares below, a patchwork of fields stretching toward the horizon, the silver ribbon of a river winding its way through the land. It was still—quiet. The kind of quiet that doesn't feel empty but full.

I remember lying down in the grass, my hands behind my head, staring at the sky as the clouds drifted by. I remember the exact shade of blue—soft, endless, something between a dream and the ocean. I remember the smell of the earth beneath me, the rustling of the wind, the distant sound of birds.

And I remember the feeling.

For the first time in my life, I felt like I was in a place where nothing was expected of me. No one needed me to be anything, to perform, to fit into any particular role. The world just was. And I just was.

I think about that place a lot. I wish I could take you there.

Maybe it's selfish, but part of me hopes that if I share this memory with you, you'll carry a piece of it with you too. Maybe you'll close your eyes and imagine it—

the way the golden grass sways in the wind, the way the sky stretches forever, the way the air smells fresh and a little bit like rain.

Maybe, for a moment, you'll feel what I felt that day.

And maybe that means I won't be alone in this memory anymore.

Do you have a place like that, You? A place where you can just exist? A place where the world doesn't ask anything of you, doesn't demand or expect, but just... lets you be?

And if you don't, I hope you find one someday.

Because sometimes, I think, we all need a place like that —a place to just be.

Until next time,

Soren

Anya closed the book slowly, her fingers lingering on the edges of the pages. The words still echoed in her mind, painting a vivid picture she could almost step into.

She could see it: the small hill outside town, the golden grass swaying in the breeze, the sky stretching endlessly overhead. She could hear the rustling of the wind, feel the cool earth beneath her palms. It wasn't just a place in Soren's memory anymore—somehow, it had become a place in hers too.

She let her eyes drift shut, allowing herself to sink into the world he had created. And then, as if her imagination had taken his words as an invitation, she saw him there too.

Soren.

She didn't know what he looked like, didn't know the sound of his voice or the way he moved, but somehow, she could feel his presence. He was lying in the grass beside her, hands behind his head, staring at the clouds with that same quiet stillness he had written about.

They didn't speak.

They didn't need to.

There was nothing to be said—no expectations to fulfill, no roles to play—just the two of them, side by side, existing in a moment that didn't belong to the past or the future.

Anya exhaled slowly, her heart aching with something she couldn't quite name. It wasn't sadness, not exactly. It was something softer, something deeper—a longing, maybe.

Or was it recognition?

Because for the first time in a long time, she realized how much she wanted a place like that too—a place where she didn't have to be anyone but herself, a place where, if she closed her eyes and listened, she could almost hear someone else breathing beside her—someone she had never met, but someone she was beginning to know.

CHAPTER : THIRTEEN

The Tenth Letter

Dear You,

I've been thinking about silence a lot lately—about all the things I've left unsaid.

There are moments I replay in my mind, conversations I wish I could rewrite, words I should have spoken. Do you ever do that? Lie awake at night, pulling old exchanges apart, searching for a different outcome? I do. All the time.

There's something about silence that haunts me.

Maybe it's because I've kept so much inside.

Maybe it's because I've watched words slip through my fingers like sand, only to wish I could gather them back and set them free before it was too late.

I remember wanting to tell someone something important—something pressing against my ribs, clawing at my throat. But I didn't. I swallowed it down, convinced it wasn't the right moment or that it wouldn't change anything.

But unsaid words don't vanish. They settle in your chest, layer after layer, until they're bricks pressing on your lungs. No matter how you try to ignore them, they stay.

I wonder—if I'd spoken back then, would I still feel the weight now?

Do you have words like that too? An apology, a confession, a goodbye? Or perhaps you were waiting for someone else to speak, and they never did, leaving a gap where their words should have been.

Maybe that's why I write these letters.

Because I want to believe words matter, that even those

left unspoken can still find a way to be heard. Even if I never know who you are, even if I never hear your voice, there's a chance these words will reach you exactly when you need them.

That uncertainty is the hardest part—not knowing whether what we say will be heard as we mean it, whether our silences are understood or mistaken for indifference. I wonder how many lives feel unfinished because someone was too afraid to speak.

If you had one moment to break a silence, what would you say?

Would it be an apology? A confession? A simple "I miss you"?

I wish I could promise that words always change things, that speaking up is always right. But sometimes words come too late or fall on unwilling ears; sometimes they only dig wounds

Then again, maybe the point isn't whether words change anything. Maybe the point is that we say them —that we don't let them rot inside us, don't let regret harden in our chests.

Maybe that's why I'm writing to you.

Because even if you never write back, even if I never hear your voice, at least I can say I tried.

At least I can say I spoke.

At least I can say silence didn't win.

And maybe, if you ever find yourself with words trapped in your heart, afraid to let them go, you'll remember this letter and speak to them anyway.

Because the alternative is so much heavier.

And you don't deserve to carry that weight alone.

Until next time,

Soren

CHAPTER : FOURTEEN

The Eleventh Letter

Dear You,

I wonder where you are right now.

Are you somewhere familiar, somewhere that feels like home? Or are you in a place unknown to me, far away from anything I could ever imagine?

I think about this more often than I should—where you might be, what your world looks like, how different your life is from mine. Maybe you're curled up in a quiet bookstore, the scent of old pages filling the air. Maybe you're on a train, watching the world blur past through the window as you hold this letter in your hands. Maybe you're somewhere by the sea, listening to waves crash against the shore, the wind tangling your hair as you turn these pages.

Or maybe you're somewhere I could never picture, somewhere I wouldn't even know existed unless you told me.

It's strange, isn't it? The way words can travel. The way they can reach places the writer has never been, never even dreamed of. The way they can find their way into someone else's life without ever asking permission.

I wonder if you stop to consider that, too—how far something has come before it reaches you, the hands it has passed through, the moments that led to this one where you sit, wherever you are, with this letter before you.

I wish I could see it.

I wish I could step into your world for just a moment, look around, breathe it in. Would I recognize it? Would it feel foreign, or would something about it seem strangely familiar?

Would I recognize you? That's the real question, isn't it?

Because even if I could see the place you're in, even if I could reach through these pages and stand next to you, would I know it was you? Would I feel it in my bones, in my chest, in that part of me that's come to believe, somehow, that we were meant to find each other like this?

Maybe.

Or maybe that's just wishful thinking.

Have you ever felt that way—like an invisible thread ties you to something, to someone, even when you can't explain it? Like you were always meant to stumble upon something at the exact moment you did?

What if you'd found this letter earlier? Would it have meant the same? Would you have picked it up or walked right past, unaware it was meant for you? And what if you'd found it later? Would it still feel like fate or like something that arrived too late?

I don't know if I believe in perfect timing, but I do believe in this: you are reading these words right now, wherever you are.

Because what matters is that this letter reaches you —that these words found their way across distances I can't see, through moments I'll never know. Somehow, despite all the chances for this never to happen, you are here. And I am here.

And now, in some quiet, impossible way, we're in the same place.

Tell me—what does it look like from where you are? Is the sky dark, stars blinking quietly above as you sit alone with these words? Or is it daylight, the world moving around you while you steal a moment to yourself? Are you warm, wrapped in a blanket with tea cooling beside you? Or are you somewhere cold, where the wind bites and you tuck this letter closer?

Are you alone? Or is someone beside you, unaware that you're lost in a conversation with someone they don't know exists?

Wherever you are, I hope it feels safe. I hope it feels like somewhere you can breathe.

And if it doesn't—if you feel far from home, far from where you're meant to be—then I hope, just for a little while, these words make you feel less alone.

That's the thing about letters, isn't it? They don't need

a perfect destination to matter. They just need to be read.

And you are reading this.

So, in a way, I'm there with you—not physically, not where you can see or touch me, but in a way that matters. In a way that reminds me that across distance and silence, words can find the person who needs them most.

And I hope, wherever you are, these words feel like home.

Until next time,

Soren

Anya exhaled, the weight of Soren's words settling deep within her. She was in her bedroom, curled on the corner of her bed, the book open on her lap. A dim lamp cast a soft glow, flickering as evening breeze slipped through the half-open window. Outside, the city hummed—cars, voices, life continuing as always.

But here, time felt paused.

Where are you right now? Soren's question lingered. She

looked around—walls lined with shelves, her worn blanket, tea on the nightstand. It was her space. Yet it felt different.

She realized she was somewhere between her world and his, between reality and the quiet intimacy of his words.

Would I recognize you? The thought sent a shiver. Would she know Soren if she passed him on the street? If he sat across from her at a café, would she feel familiarity? Or does this connection exist only in ink and paper?

She traced the inked letters.

> *"And I hope, wherever you are, that these words feel like home."*

She closed the book and pressed it to her chest. He didn't know where she was. Yet, somehow, impossibly, he had found her anyway.

And maybe, just maybe, that was enough.

CHAPTER : FIFTEEN

The Twelfth Letter

Dear You,

There's a peculiar kind of intimacy in the space between what is spoken and what remains unsaid—a hidden layer of understanding that exists not in the physical presence of another, but in the resonance of words, in the silent echoes that follow each phrase. I think I know you, even if I don't, because the act of writing these letters has allowed me to paint an image of you from nothing more than the quiet spaces in my own heart, and in that process I have discovered that words can bridge distances the senses cannot reach.

I remember a time when I believed that knowing someone meant sharing physical moments—touches, glances, voices rising and falling in laughter. I believed that to truly know another, one had to stand close enough to see the subtle tremble of their hands, the fleeting glimmer in their eyes when something moved them deeply. But as I sit here writing to you, I real-

ize that I know you in a way that defies the need for physical presence. In the quiet solitude of my thoughts, I have come to see you as a mosaic of hopes, fears, dreams, and unspoken truths—a collection of nuances and delicate imperfections that form the essence of who you are.

It's a strange idea: that I might know you through the shared language of emotion and memory, that even though our lives have never crossed paths, our inner worlds can converse in a dialect beyond words. Perhaps it is the magic of this written form—a kind of alchemy that transforms simple ink into a medium for connection. In every letter I write, I reach into the darkness, hoping my words will find you and speak to you in the language of understanding.

I imagine that you, too, carry within you a secret library of memories, a collection of experiences that have shaped you into the person you are now. I imagine that you have felt joy so profound it brought tears to your eyes, pain so deep it left an indelible mark on your soul, and moments of quiet wonder that made you believe that even in the midst of chaos there is beauty to be found. And although I have never seen these memories first hand, I feel them in the cadence of your silence, in the spaces between my own thoughts when I pause to consider all that remains unsaid.

Sometimes, as I write, I wonder if you ever feel the

same—a silent understanding that transcends the need for words spoken aloud. It is in these moments that I become convinced true connection does not always demand familiarity, that knowing someone deeply can occur in the quiet exchange of vulnerabilities captured on paper. In these letters, I confess pieces of myself I have long kept hidden, and, in doing so, I extend an invitation to you: to see me, to understand me, and in that understanding perhaps to see a reflection of your own soul.

I have learned there is beauty in imperfection, in the raw honesty that emerges when we strip away our pretenses and reveal our true selves. I have learned that the unspoken truths—the tears we never cry out loud, the laughter we reserve for the quiet corners of our hearts—can speak louder than any well-rehearsed conversation. And so, as I write to you

Now, I offer you a glimpse into my inner world, trusting that in the exchange of these letters we might both find solace and connection.

There are moments when I imagine us sitting across from one another in a small café or on a park bench, each of us enveloped in our own quiet reflections. I picture you listening intently as I share my thoughts, your eyes reflecting a calm understanding that tells me you, too, have wrestled with the mysteries of love, loss, hope, and despair. While I know such physical meetings may never come to pass, the thought itself is comforting; it tells me that even if our bodies never touch, our minds and hearts can still meet in the vast expanse of time and space.

I wonder—do you ever feel the pull of memories, those fleeting images of childhood laughter, of warm summer evenings when the world seemed limitless, of whispered promises made under starlit skies? I do; I do with every beat of my heart and with every word I commit to this page. Despite the uncertainty and vulnerability that come with it, I offer you this question as both a confession and a prayer—a prayer that you might one day feel the warmth of connection I so desperately seek, a warmth that transcends the boundaries of physical presence and enters the realm of the spirit.

Until I hear, even silently, that you think of me too, I will continue to write these letters, to share these fragments of my soul in the hope that somewhere in the depths of your thoughts my words find a home. I will write with the earnest belief that our hearts, no matter how far apart, can converse in the gentle language of longing and remembrance.

I leave you with this, dear You, as a final thought in this letter: if, in a moment of quiet reflection, you ever find yourself wondering if someone, somewhere, holds you in their thoughts, know that I am that someone. And if you, too, allow yourself the freedom to hope and to feel, perhaps you will realize that in the vast tapestry of our lives, the threads of our hearts might be woven together —however subtly—to form a connection as real as it is fragile.

With all the quiet understanding my heart can muster,

Soren

Anya sat in the dim glow of her bedside lamp, the letter still open in her hands, her fingers resting lightly on the edge of the page. The world outside her window was silent, but inside her there was a hum—a quiet resonance, as if something deep within her had stirred. Soren's words had reached her in a way she hadn't expected, slipping past the careful walls she had built around herself. She exhaled, feeling an odd sense of warmth and weightlessness at the same time. I think I know you, even if I don't. The sentence repeated in her mind, threading itself through the fabric of her thoughts. It was strange, how someone who had never seen her, never heard the sound of her voice, could describe something so intimate—so achingly familiar. It was as if he had pulled the thoughts straight from her own heart and laid them bare on the page.

For the first time, she allowed herself to wonder—who was Soren? What kind of person could write with such depth, such understanding? Did he truly mean the words he wrote, or was this just an illusion, a carefully woven dream she had let herself sink into? And yet, despite the questions—despite the uncertainty—she couldn't deny how his words made her feel: seen, heard, understood.

She traced the last few lines with her eyes, her lips pressing together.

> *"Until next time, know that I am here, listening to the silent music of your soul ..."*

Anya leaned back against the headboard, closing her eyes for a brief moment. There was something terrifying about how much she wanted to believe those words —how much she wished they were meant for her alone. But wasn't that the beauty of it? Somehow, in the space between strangers, in the quiet of ink and paper, she had found a connection that felt as real as anything she had ever known.

CHAPTER : SIXTEEN

The Thirteenth Letter

Dear You,

There's a strange comfort in writing to you.

I never thought I would find comfort in something as simple as writing to someone I've never met, and yet here I am, looking forward to these letters as if they are conversations between old friends. It's strange, isn't it? How words—just ink on paper (or thoughts turned into keystrokes, depending on how you imagine this)—can feel like a real connection.

I wonder if you feel it too.

Maybe it's just me, pouring out thoughts that would otherwise remain locked away, but there's something deeply satisfying about writing to you. It's different from talking to a friend, different from journaling, different from anything else I've known. A letter is both personal and distant, intimate yet safe. I can tell you things I wouldn't say out loud, and yet it doesn't feel like I'm speaking into a void; it feels like you're listening.

And that is comforting.

Have you ever felt that way before—that kind of quiet comfort in something small? Maybe in the way you hold a warm cup of tea between your hands on a cold morning, or in the way rain taps softly against your window at night, or in the familiarity of an old song you've played a hundred times before that still makes you feel something new each time.

That's what writing to you feels like.

At first, I didn't think these letters would mean much. I thought they'd be a fleeting experiment—just words sent out into the unknown. But now I find myself looking forward to them. I don't even know if you're reading them, but that doesn't seem to matter. It's the act of writing itself that brings me peace. Maybe it's because, in these moments, I'm not just a person lost in a crowd; I'm someone writing to someone.

And that makes all the difference.

I don't think we realize how much we need to be heard until we find a way to express ourselves. Most of the time, we walk through life carrying thoughts too heavy to speak, feelings too fragile to share. We convince ourselves that no one will understand—or worse, that no one will care. But what if that isn't true? What if we're all just waiting for someone to listen?

That's what I wonder about sometimes.

There's a strange kind of vulnerability in writing to you —not because I fear being judged (you don't even know who I am) but because it forces me to be honest in a way I rarely am with myself. When I write these letters, there's no need for pretense, no need to impress or prove anything. It's just me, speaking to you as if you already understand.

And maybe you do.

Maybe that's why I keep writing.

I wonder what kind of person you are. Are you the kind who reads slowly, savoring every word, or do you skim through letters, catching only the important parts? Do you pause to think about what I've written, or do you let the words wash over you like waves, moving past them as soon as they've been read?

I don't mind either way. The fact that you're here—that you've made it this far—is enough.

I imagine you sometimes. Not your face, because I don't know what you look like, but your presence. I picture you sitting by a window, reading this letter with a thoughtful expression. Maybe you're alone, or maybe the distant hum of life surrounds you—people talking, cars passing, the faint sound of music playing somewhere in the background.

I wonder if you're the kind of person who loves silence or if you find it unsettling. I think about whether you read these letters at night, just before sleep, or in the quiet moments of the morning when the world is still waking up.

Maybe I'll never know.

But there's something beautiful in that mystery, don't you think? The not-knowing, the endless possibilities. It means I can imagine you however I want, and in some way, you can do the same with me.

I think that's part of why these letters feel so comfort-

ing: they exist in a space beyond reality, beyond expectations. In this place, there are no awkward pauses, no misunderstandings, no need to explain ourselves—just words flowing freely between us, connecting us in a way that is both real and not real at the same time.

Maybe that's why I don't want to stop writing.

Even though I don't know where these letters will lead, I find myself unwilling to let go. There's something about them that feels necessary, as if they are filling a space I didn't even know was empty.

Have you ever felt that way about something?

Like finding an old book in a second-hand shop, one that seems to have been waiting just for you, or stumbling upon a song that feels like it was written for a moment you didn't even know you needed it for. That's what these letters are becoming for me—a quiet presence, a steady rhythm in the chaos of life. I wonder if they will become that for you too.

Maybe they already have.

Maybe, like me, you've found a strange kind of comfort in them—in knowing that someone, somewhere, is writing to you with no expectation, no demands. Just the simple act of reaching out, of sharing thoughts that might otherwise be lost to time.

I like that idea.

So I will keep writing.

Because even if these letters are never read—even if they are nothing more than words floating into the unknown—they will still have mattered. They are real to me, and in some way, I hope they are real to you too.

Until next time,

Me

CHAPTER : SEVENTEEN

Anya felt honesty in Soren's writing—the kind that wasn't polished or rehearsed but raw, unfiltered, and real. It was as if he wasn't just writing words; he was unraveling pieces of himself with every sentence. She could almost hear his voice in her head—not in a literal sense, but in the way his words carried emotions, in the rhythm of his thoughts.

She leaned back in her chair, staring at the letter for a long moment. It was strange, wasn't it, to feel connected to someone whose face she didn't know, whose name remained a mystery? And yet, as she read through his words again, she realized something—she didn't need to know those things. His presence was already there, woven into the letters he wrote.

Soren spoke of finding comfort in these letters, but what about her? Had she also found a strange kind of comfort in reading them? She traced a finger over the edge of the page, considering that thought. It wasn't just the letters themselves; it was the way he noticed things—small, fleeting moments that most people overlooked: the warmth of a cup in cold hands, the rhythm of rain against a window, the familiarity of an old song.

Anya knew those feelings well.

Anya couldn't keep the book down.

She told herself she would stop after this letter—just one more, just to see where his thoughts led him. But as her eyes reached the last words, her fingers hesitated before closing the pages. The weight of his honesty, the quiet intimacy in his words, held her in place.

It was strange, wasn't it, how a book—just ink on paper—could make her feel like someone was speaking directly to her? Not in the distant way most stories did, but in a way that felt immediate, personal, as if Soren was sitting across from her, waiting for her to respond.

She wasn't sure why she cared so much. She didn't even know him. And yet, she felt a small, unexpected ache at the thought of him writing without knowing if anyone was reading—without knowing that she was reading.

A part of her wanted to say something. But to whom? The letters had no return address. There was no way to reach him, no way to let him know that his words hadn't been lost to the void.

And maybe that was the point.

Anya exhaled softly, glancing toward the clock. It was later than she thought, but sleep felt like a distant possibility now. The book was still warm in her hands, as if it had been waiting for her all along.
Just one more.

CHAPTER : EIGHTEEN

The Fourteenth Letter

Dear You,

I find myself thinking about it more often than I should —this idea of us, somewhere else, in some other time. It's a strange thought, isn't it? The possibility that, in another life under different circumstances, we might have met in a way that was entirely ordinary yet completely extraordinary.

I wonder how it would have happened.

Would we have passed each other on a crowded street, our shoulders barely brushing as we moved in opposite directions, never realizing the weight of that fleeting moment? Or would it have been something more—something that stopped time for just a second, something that made us look twice?

I like to imagine different versions of us.

Maybe, in one life, we are strangers on a train, sitting across from each other, both lost in our own thoughts. You would be reading a book, and I would pretend not to notice, but I'd catch myself wondering what kind of stories you liked. Would you glance up at me—just for a second—before returning to your page? Or would I be the one to break the silence, asking about the title, hoping it would lead to something more?

Maybe, in another life, we meet in a bookstore. You're standing in the poetry section, your fingers tracing the worn-out spine of an old book, and I watch from a distance, wondering what kind of words make your heartache in the best way. I would wait, pretending to be interested in something else, and when you finally walked away, I'd take the book you left behind, reading the same lines you had just touched.

Or maybe we met as children, long before the world taught us how to build walls around ourselves. Maybe we were the kind of kids who spent summers chasing sunsets, racing the waves at the shore, laughing over things we wouldn't remember years later. Maybe we made promises to always stay in touch—the way children do before they understand how life pulls people apart. Would we have kept those promises, or would we have become a distant memory, a name remembered in passing?

And then there's the possibility that we were something more than strangers in another life.

What if we were best friends—the kind who stayed up all night talking about dreams that felt too big, too impossible, yet still dared to believe in them together? The kind who knew each other better than we knew ourselves, who could tell how the other was feeling just by the way they sighed? Maybe we had inside jokes that made no coffee, the songs that make you nostalgic, the way you tuck your hair behind your ear when you're deep in thought.

What if we were lovers?

What if, in another life, I had already traced the shape of your smile a hundred times? What if I had memorized the way your voice changes when you're tired—the way you whisper secrets as if the world might steal them away? What if we had shared the kind of love that felt effortless, the kind that made even the most ordinary days feel like something out of a story?

Would we have been happy?

Would we have found a way to make it last, or would we have fallen apart the way some people do, despite loving each other the best way they knew how? Would we have fought over the little things—forgotten anniversaries, unanswered messages, the weight of expectations? Or would we have been the kind of people who always found their way back to each other, no matter how lost they became?

I don't know.

I imagine there are times when you feel the pull of nostalgia—when a song on the radio or the scent of rain triggers a cascade of memories that make you wonder about the roads not taken, the conversations never had, the words left unsaid. In those moments, do you ever pause to think of a stranger who dares to write—who dares to hope his thoughts might resonate with your own? Do you ever feel, even for a fleeting moment, that perhaps our lives, though lived separately, are intertwined in a way that defies explanation?

I do. I do with every beat of my heart and with every word I commit to this page. And so, despite the uncertainty and the vulnerability that comes with it, I offer you this question as both a confession and a prayer—a prayer that you might one day feel the warmth of connection I so desperately seek, a warmth that transcends the boundaries of physical presence and enters the realm of the spirit.

Until I hear, even silently, that you think of me too, I will continue to write these letters—to share these fragments of my soul in the hope that somewhere, in the depths of your thoughts, my words find a home. I will write with the earnest belief that our hearts, no matter how far apart, can converse in the gentle language of longing and remembrance.

I leave you with this, dear You, as a final thought in this letter: if, in a moment of quiet reflection, you ever find yourself wondering if someone, somewhere, holds you in their thoughts, know that I am that someone. And if you, too, allow yourself the freedom to hope and to feel, perhaps you will realize that in the vast tapestry of our lives the threads of our hearts might be woven together —however subtly—to form a connection that is as real as it is fragile. I await that understanding with a heart full of hope and a pen that continues to write, even when the night seems too dark. May these words serve as a gentle reminder that you are not alone in your thoughts, and that somewhere, I am thinking of you too.

Soren

Anya's fingers trembled slightly as she turned the page, her breath shallow, as if exhaling too loudly might shatter the moment. She had been prepared for another letter, another carefully crafted string of words that would tug at something deep inside her—but this? This was different. Her fingers curled around the edges of the book, gripping it as if it might slip from her hands. Her eyes traced the words again, lingering on one line longer than she should have.

What if we were lovers?

A shiver ran down her spine, and she swallowed hard, as if that alone could steady the sudden, unsteady rhythm of her heart. It was just a question—one of many scattered throughout the letter—but it felt different, more intimate, more dangerous.

She shouldn't be reacting like this.

It was just ink on paper, just a stranger's thoughts, written without ever knowing she would read them. And yet, something about the way he had written it, the quiet longing threaded between the words, made it impossible to ignore.

What if, in another life, I had already traced the shape of your smile a hundred times?

Anya exhaled, slow and uneven, feeling warmth creep up her neck. It was unsettling—the way these letters reached into places she had never expected, how they made her feel seen in ways she couldn't explain.

She closed the book for a moment, pressing her fingers against the cover as if that could steady her, but it was already too late. The words had settled deep, refusing to leave her.

And the worst part?

A part of her wanted to believe it.

CHAPTER : NINETEEN

The Fifteenth Letter

Dear You,

I should stop.

I know that.

This started as something simple—a quiet act of putting my thoughts into words, like dropping letters into an ocean with no expectation of them ever reaching the shore. It was supposed to be nothing more than a passing thought, a way to speak without speaking, to confess things I wouldn't say out loud.

But now, it's something more.

I don't know when it happened, but these letters aren't just words anymore. They aren't just thoughts I scatter into the void, hoping they disappear. They have become something I look forward to—something I need.

I should stop.

But I won't.

Because the truth is, I like writing to you.

I like the way my mind settles when I sit down and start another letter. I like the way the words pour out, the way they feel honest in a way spoken words never do. It's strange, isn't it? How easy it is to say things here that I wouldn't say if you were sitting in front of me.

Maybe that's why I keep going.

Maybe that's why I can't stop.

Because in these letters, I am more myself than I ever am in real life. I don't have to pretend. I don't have to hold back.

I can be quiet without being overlooked.

I can be honest without fear.

I can be seen, even without being known.

There's a kind of freedom in that—writing to someone who may or may not be there, knowing my words exist whether or not they're ever read. It makes me wonder... if I stopped writing, would it feel like losing something real?

Because this is real, in its own way.

You are real—even if I've never heard your voice, even if I don't know the sound of your laughter or the way you furrow your brow when you're lost in thought, even if I don't know your name.

And that's the strangest part of all: how real you feel to me.

I don't know who you are, and yet I write to you like I've known you forever.

It's terrifying.

It's also the easiest thing I've ever done.

Maybe that's why I don't want to stop.

Because if I do, what happens to all the things I still haven't said? What happens to the thoughts that only make sense when I put them here, between the lines of these letters? What happens to the parts of me that only exist when I write them down?

I don't have an answer to that.

And maybe that's why I keep writing—because there's comfort in knowing that, as long as I keep putting my words on these pages, a part of me will always exist in them; that even if you never find them, even if they never reach you, they are still here. And that's enough. Or at least, it should be.

But sometimes I wonder—do you ever wish you could write back?

Do you ever feel the urge to respond—to leave some-

thing behind, even if it's just a single word? Do you ever imagine what you might say to me, if given the chance?

Would you tell me your name?

Would you tell me about your day—the little moments you thought weren't worth mentioning to anyone else?

Would you ask me to keep writing?

Or would you tell me to stop?

I don't know.

And maybe I'll never know.

But it doesn't change the fact that, no matter what, I won't stop.

Because somewhere along the way, these letters became more than just thoughts written down; they became a part of me.

And I'm not ready to let go of that just yet.

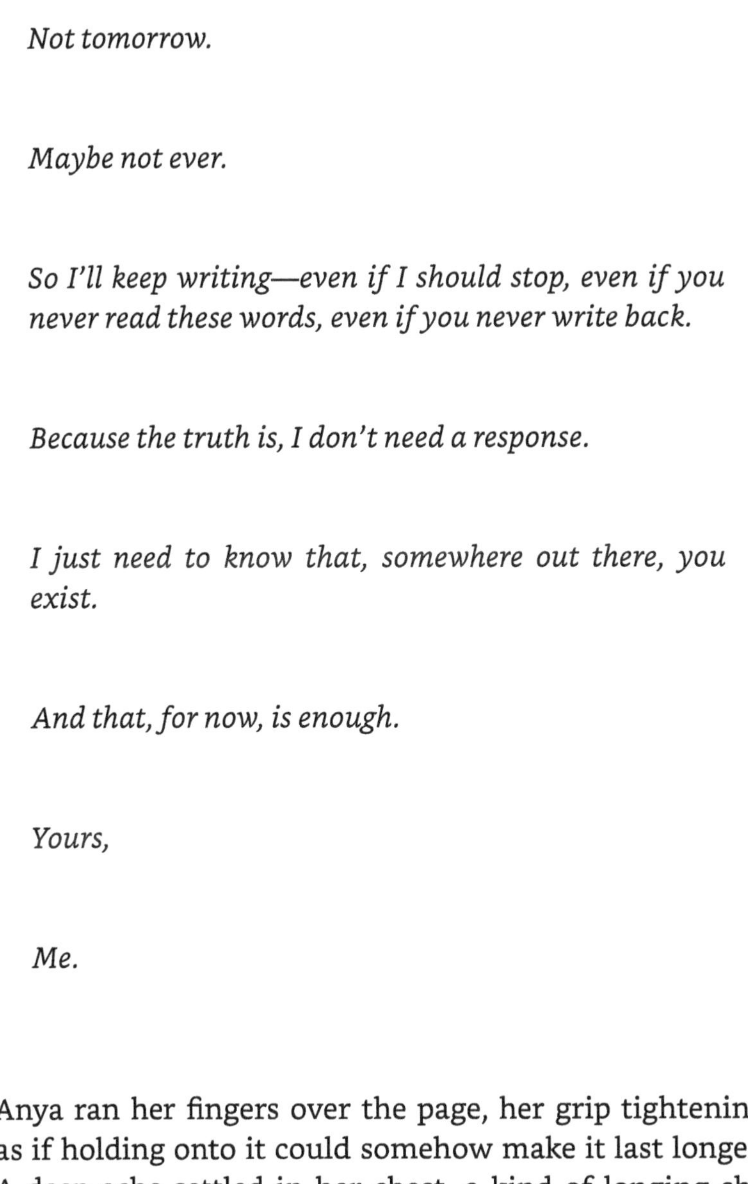

Not tomorrow.

Maybe not ever.

So I'll keep writing—even if I should stop, even if you never read these words, even if you never write back.

Because the truth is, I don't need a response.

I just need to know that, somewhere out there, you exist.

And that, for now, is enough.

Yours,

Me.

Anya ran her fingers over the page, her grip tightening as if holding onto it could somehow make it last longer. A deep ache settled in her chest, a kind of longing she couldn't quite name.

He should stop—that's what he said—but he wouldn't.

And, for reasons she couldn't explain, that meant everything.

She exhaled slowly, feeling the weight of his words press against her. The quiet honesty, the rawness of it—it was unlike anything she had ever read before. These letters weren't just words on a page; they weren't just thoughts spilled into the void—they were him, his mind, his heart, laid bare for someone he didn't even know.

For her.

Did he realize how much he had given away? Did he know how vulnerable he sounded—or was that the very reason he kept writing? Because these letters were a space where he could be seen without the fear of recognition.

Anya traced a finger over the ink, her throat tightening. He wondered if she ever wanted to write back—if she ever wanted to respond, even with a single word.

Yes.

She wanted to tell him yes.

She wanted to tell him that she read every letter as if it were meant for her alone, that somewhere between the lines, between the quiet confessions and hesitant admissions, she had started waiting for them—hoping for them.

She wanted to tell him not to stop. Not because he needed to keep writing for her, but
finding no new words, no new thoughts, no new pieces of him spilled onto a page—she couldn't bear it.

Anya swallowed hard and closed the book, but the words lingered.

What if we were lovers?

The thought crept in, unbidden, startling her. It was ridiculous—impossible—they had never met; she didn't even know his name.

And yet, despite telling herself she would stop for now, despite trying so many times to set the book aside and take a breath, she found herself turning the page—unable to help it, unable to stop. She kept reading, one letter after another, as if his words had become something she couldn't let go of.

CHAPTER : TWENTY

The Sixteenth Letter

Dear You,

What Does Love Feel Like?

I've been avoiding this question.

Not because I don't want to answer it, but because I'm afraid of what the answer might be.

What does love feel like?

I've asked myself this before, but never in a way that mattered. It was always an abstract thought—something distant, meant for other people. I used to think love was a grand, sweeping thing—loud and obvious, something that made itself known the moment it arrived. But now I'm starting to wonder if love is quieter than that.

If it isn't something that crashes into you like a wave, but rather something that seeps into the spaces between your ribs, unnoticed, until one day you realize it's been there all along.

Because the truth is... I don't know when it started.

I don't know the exact moment I began writing to you differently—when these letters became something more than just words on a page. I don't know when I stopped addressing them to no one and started addressing them to you.

But I know that I did.

And now I can't stop wondering.

Is this love?

Is love the way I think about you before I fall asleep, even though I don't know your face?
Is love the way I write these letters with the quiet hope

that, wherever you are, you might feel them?
Is love the way my chest feels lighter when I put these words down, as if writing to you is the one thing that makes sense in a world that often doesn't?

Or is this something else entirely?

Maybe love isn't something that can be defined so easily. Maybe it isn't just one feeling, but a collection of them—something that builds slowly, piece by piece, until you can't ignore it anymore. Maybe it's the comfort of knowing someone exists, even if you've never met them. Maybe it's the way your heart lingers on the thought of

Maybe love is this.

Or maybe I'm just getting lost in my own words again.

I shouldn't be thinking about this.
I shouldn't be writing this.

And yet here I am, wondering if it's possible to love someone you've never met—wondering if feelings can exist in the space between words, in the quiet between letters.

Because if love is something you feel—something that changes the way you see the world—then maybe I am feeling it.

Maybe I have been for a while now.

I used to think love required something tangible—touch, presence, time spent together in the same space. But what if love also exists beyond those things? What if love can be found in a name never spoken, in a voice never heard, in a connection that exists only through ink on paper?

Would that make it any less real?

I don't know. I don't know if this is love.

But I do know that you matter to me.

And that scares me more than I'd like to admit.

Because if I've learned anything, it's that love—no matter how it comes—is dangerous. It makes people vulnerable. It makes them hope, makes them long for things they might never have, makes them dream of impossible things.

And I... I'm afraid of that.

Because what happens if I wake up one day and realize that I've built something out of nothing—that I've fallen for a ghost, for a presence that only exists in these letters? What happens if I never hear from you, never find proof that you're out there reading these words?

Will I still feel this way?

Will you?

I wish I knew the answer.

I wish I knew what love was supposed to feel like so I could be sure of what this is.

But maybe that's the thing about love—maybe it isn't something you can define. Maybe it's just something you know when you feel it, even if you don't fully understand it.

And right now, I feel something.

Something I can't quite name.
Something that keeps me writing to you, even when I tell myself to stop.
Something that makes me wonder if you ever think of me the way I think of you—something that makes me want to believe in the impossible, just for a little while longer.

So tell me...

If this was love, would it feel any different?
Would I know?
Would you?

I don't have an answer.

But I do know this—

I should stop writing this letter.
I should stop thinking about you this way.
I should stop wondering what your voice sounds like, what your laughter would feel like if I ever heard it.
I should stop imagining the way you might smile while reading this—stop pretending that these words mean

something to you the way they mean something to me.

But I won't.

I can't.

Because the truth is, no matter what this is—love, longing, or just a foolish attachment to someone I'll never meet—

I don't want to let it go.

Not yet.
Not now.
Maybe not ever.

So I'll keep writing.

Even if I never get an answer.
Even if you never know.
Even if these words are all I'll ever have.

Because maybe love isn't about what you receive in return.
Maybe love is just the act of giving—of sending some-

thing out into the world and hoping that, somehow, it finds its way to the right person.And if that's true... then I think I already know my answer.

Yours,

Me

Anya's breath caught as she reached the end of the letter. Her heart skipped a beat—just once, but enough for her to notice. She shouldn't feel this way; she shouldn't let words on a page make her feel as if they were meant for her.

And yet, they did.

Before she could stop herself—before she could reason with the part of her that told her to pause, to breathe, to step away—her fingers moved on their own. She turned the page, unable to resist the pull of what lay ahead.

CHAPTER : TWENTY-ONE

The Seventeenth Letter

Dear You,

If I Describe You, Will It Sound Like I Know You?

I don't know what you look like.

I don't know the sound of your voice, the way you laugh, or the little expressions you make when you're deep in thought. I don't know if your hands are calloused from work or soft from days spent between pages of a book; I don't know if you like the way your hair falls in the morning, if you trace patterns absent-mindedly on your skin when you're thinking, or if you talk to yourself when no one else is around.

But if I describe you, will it sound like I do?

Because I think I do.

I think you're the kind of person who notices small things—like the way sunlight filters through the trees in late afternoon or the way rain smells just before it starts to fall. I think you're the kind of person who remembers details about people, even when they don't realize it. Maybe you remember birthdays without needing a reminder, or notice when someone's mood shifts by the way they sigh.

I think you stare at the sky more than most people—not just when it's clear and blue, but when it's stormy too, when the clouds are heavy and rolling, when lightning flickers in the distance, when the world feels on the edge of something. I think you understand that beauty isn't always in the perfect, but in the things that change, in the things that carry stories within them.

I think you love the quiet.

Not silence—true silence can be deafening—but the kind of quiet that comes with familiarity: the stillness of an early morning before the world wakes, the hush of a bookstore when everyone is lost in their own worlds, the comfort of being next to someone and not needing to fill the space with words.

I think you're the kind of person who listens—really listens. Not just to words, but to what's left unspoken. You notice the weight behind someone's voice, the hesitation in their pauses, the way their hands fidget when they're trying to hold something back. You understand that sometimes people don't need advice; they just need to be heard.

I think you love deeply, even if you don't always say it out loud. Maybe you show it in small ways: in the way you save the last bite of your favorite food for someone else, in the way you check in on people even when they seem fine, in the way you hold onto memories, keeping them tucked away in the quiet corners of your heart, I think you have a complicated relationship with love. Maybe you've been hurt before; maybe you've given your heart to people who didn't know how to hold it. Maybe you're afraid

of love slipping through your fingers—of it being something fleeting instead of something that stays. Maybe you don't believe in love the way others do—not the grand, sweeping, fairy-tale kind, but the quiet kind, the kind that lingers, the kind that doesn't ask for much, only to be felt.

I think you dream of things you're too afraid to say out loud. You have hopes, secrets, desires that you keep close to your chest, fearing they might crumble if ex-

posed to the world. Maybe you've told yourself that some dreams are too big, too impossible, too foolish. But I hope you haven't given up on them; I hope you still believe, even if only a little.

I think you long for something, even if you don't know what it is—a place that feels like home, a love that feels like certainty, a feeling you can't quite name but that you're always reaching for, hoping that one day you'll find it.

I don't know your name. I don't know your face. But I know that you are more than just a person who happened upon these letters.

You are someone who reads between the lines.
You are someone who feels.
You are someone who lingers in the spaces where others rush through.

And that tells me more about you than any photograph ever could.

Maybe I don't know you the way the world defines knowing. But if knowing someone is about understanding the parts of them they don't always show—about seeing them in the way they move through the world rather than the way the world sees them—then maybe

I do know you.

Or maybe... maybe I'm just hoping that someone like you exists.

And if you do—if I've described you in ways that feel true, in ways that make you pause, in ways that make you wonder how a stranger could put into words the things you've never spoken—then maybe I was always meant to write to you. Maybe you were always meant to find this. Maybe, in some strange, inexplicable way, we were always meant to meet here—between the ink and the spaces in between.

Tell me—did I get you right? Or did I only describe the parts of you that you've never dared to say out loud?

Yours,

Always

Anya sat cross-legged on her bed, the book of letters resting against her lap. The soft glow of her bedside lamp cast long shadows across the room, its golden light the only source of warmth in the otherwise quiet night. She had been meaning to sleep; she had told herself she would stop after just one more letter.

And now, she couldn't look away. Her fingers traced the edges of the paper as she read the words again—slower this time—letting them sink in. The weight of them pressed against her ribs, delicate yet heavy, something that both soothed and unsettled her.

If I describe you, will it sound like I know you?

Anya exhaled shakily, tucking her knees closer to her chest. A cool breeze slipped in through the half-open window, rustling the curtains, but she barely noticed.

How could someone who had never met her, never seen her, never even known her name, write something that felt like a mirror?

She ran a hand through her hair, staring at the words as if they might change under her gaze.

I think you stare at the sky more than most people.

Her lips parted slightly.

How many times had she done that—standing at the window during thunderstorms, watching dark clouds swirl like ink in water; sitting on the rooftop at dusk, tracing constellations with her fingertips; getting lost in the way the sun painted the world in gold just before it dipped below the horizon?

She had never told anyone that.

And yet, here it was, written in ink, as if someone had been watching her all this time.

A shiver ran down her spine—not of fear, but of something deeper, something she couldn't quite name. She pulled her blanket tighter around her shoulders, as if it might shield her from the intensity of what she was feeling.

The room was quiet, save for the ticking of the clock on the wall. 2:17 a.m.

She should sleep.

She should close the book, place it on her nightstand, and let it rest until morning.

But her hands wouldn't let go.

She pressed her thumb against the page, her pulse thrumming beneath her skin.

> *"I think you love deeply, even if you don't always say it out loud."*

Her throat tightened.

How did he know? Anya had never been the kind of person who spilled her heart easily. She loved in quiet ways, in the little things—saving the last bite of something for someone else, remembering the songs people liked, checking in even when they She had always thought that kind of love went unnoticed.

But here it was.

Someone had noticed.

Or maybe… maybe he hadn't.

Maybe he was only writing to a faceless, nameless reader, casting his words into the unknown, hoping they would land somewhere—with someone.

And yet, they had landed here.

With her.

Anya let out a slow breath, rubbing her thumb absently over the ink.

> *"Tell me—did I get you right?"*

She wanted to answer.

She wanted to say, Yes. Yes, you did.

But to whom?

To the book? To the nameless writer? To the night itself?

She glanced at the window again. The world outside was quiet, sleeping. She wondered if, somewhere out there, the person who had written these words was awake too, wondering if someone like her existed.

Maybe that was the strangest part of all—this feeling of being connected to someone she had never met through nothing but ink and paper.

She swallowed, blinking back the emotions pressing behind her eyes. Slowly, carefully, she folded the corner of the page—marking it, as if to say, I was here. I read this. I felt this.

Then, with a deep breath, she closed the book and held it against her chest.

Maybe she didn't have answers.

Maybe she didn't need them.

But she knew one thing for certain.

She would keep reading.

CHAPTER : TWENTY-TWO

The Eighteenth Letter

Dear You,

There are moments—quiet, unassuming moments—when I find myself caught between hope and uncertainty, and I wonder: do you think of me too? I hesitate even to ask, as if the very question might shatter the fragile barrier we have built with these letters. Yet, here I am, writing these words in the hope that somewhere, across the vast expanse of time and space, you might feel the same. I have often sat in the quiet darkness of my room, the only light coming from a small lamp that casts long shadows on the wall, and my mind drifts to thoughts of you. In these moments, I am overwhelmed by a longing—a yearning to know if the feelings I carry are shared by someone I have never seen, whose presence exists only in the lines of my writing.

I remember the first time I felt this stirring within me.

It was an ordinary day—a day filled with the usual routines, the monotony of work, and the gentle hum of everyday life. And yet, as I walked home, my thoughts turned inward, drifting toward the memory of the words I had written in a previous letter. In that quiet, reflective space, a single question began to take shape: Do you think of me too? I wasn't sure whether it was a question meant for my own ears or a gentle call into the void, but as the thought persisted, it blossomed into a desire—a desire to reach out to you, to create a connection that transcended the limitations of our separate lives.

Sometimes, I find myself imagining what it would be like if we could share a conversation face-to-face. I imagine sitting in a cozy café or strolling through a quiet park, our voices mingling as we share our hopes, our fears, and the little details that make us who we are. I wonder if you, too, have moments when you pause and let your mind wander to a place where you imagine our paths crossing, even if only in the realm of dreams. Do you ever feel the gentle pull of curiosity about the person on the other end of these letters? I ask myself this repeatedly as I trace the words on the page, each line a piece of my heart laid bare, hoping that somewhere you might catch a glimpse of the emotions that swirl around me.

I often think about the nature of connection—the kind that forms not from shared laughter in the same room, but from the intimate act of confiding secrets to a kin-

dred spirit, even if that spirit exists only in the ink of written words. There is a strange beauty in knowing that, despite the distance between us, a single thought or emotion can ripple out and reach someone who feels it too. I wonder if you, in your quiet moments, feel a similar pull—if you sometimes lie awake at night, tracing memories and dreams, and pause to wonder whether someone, somewhere, is thinking of you with the same intensity. Do you recall a moment—a fleeting thought—when you wondered whether there was someone who understood the silent language of your heart?

In many ways, I am a creature of solitude, finding solace in the silent cadence of my own thoughts. Yet, in the midst of that solitude, I have discovered an unexpected comfort in writing to you. It is as if, through these letters, I have carved out a space where I am not entirely alone—a space where the echo of your existence makes the darkness feel a little less overwhelming. And so I write, not with the expectation of an answer or a response, but with the hope that my words might find resonance in the chambers of your heart. I write because I need to know that somewhere, beyond the reach of ordinary life, there is someone who feels the same weight of longing, the same bittersweet mix of hope and melancholy, that I do.

Sometimes I picture you, wherever you might be, engaged in your own quiet moments of reflection. Perhaps you are curled up in a worn armchair with a cup of tea, the steam rising in delicate curls as you read these words. Maybe you are sitting by a window, watching the rain trace gentle patterns on the glass, lost in thoughts that echo my own. In these imaginings, I do not presume to know you—I know nothing of your appearance or the details of your life—but I dare to believe that our inner worlds, so full of unspoken dreams and secret sorrows, might share a similar language. And, in that shared language, there lies the possibility of understanding, even if we have never met.

There is a vulnerability in asking whether you think of me too. It is a vulnerability born of the fear of being unreciprocated—a fear that my quiet hopes might be as solitary as the nights I spend wrestling with my own thoughts. I confess that I sometimes wonder if these letters are merely echoes in an empty chamber, if I am talking to the silence instead of to you. Yet even as that fear whispers in my ear, I find myself unable to silence the desire to reach out. I write because, despite the uncertainty, I am compelled by the possibility that you, too, might be seeking a connection that transcends the physical and reaches deep into the realm of the heart.

Do you, in moments of introspection, think about the people who have touched your life in ways both significant and subtle? Do you remember the faces that pass by in the crowd—the fleeting interactions that, though brief, leave an indelible mark on your soul? I wonder if you carry these memories with you like cherished secrets locked away in the recesses of your mind. Perhaps, when the world feels too heavy, you find comfort in recalling a kind word, a gentle smile, or even the shared silence with a stranger who, for a moment, made you feel understood. And I ask myself: could I be one of those gentle presences in your memory, even if only through the intimacy of these letters?

I imagine a scenario where, in another time or place, our paths might have crossed more tangibly. Perhaps, in that alternate reality, we would have shared stories face to face, exchanging glances that spoke volumes, filling the spaces between words with unspoken understanding. The thought of that possibility sends shivers down my spine—a mix of hope and bittersweet sorrow for what might have been. Yet, within the reality of these pages, I find comfort in the idea that even if our meeting remains confined to the realm of written words, it is no less meaningful. For in each carefully crafted sentence, in every pause laden with unspoken emotion, I sense the whisper of your existence and dare to believe that I am not the only one who clings to these fragile connections.

There is a paradox in this act of writing—a paradox where the more I try to articulate my feelings, the more elusive they become. Words, by their nature, seem inadequate to capture the full spectrum of what I feel. They flutter just out of reach, like fireflies on a warm summer night, glowing softly in the darkness before vanishing into the void. And yet I persist. I persist because I believe that even if words cannot fully en-

compass the depth of my emotions, they still serve as a beacon—a small, shining light that reaches out and touches the soul of another. So I ask again, with a hesitant heart and trembling pen: do you think of me too?

I ask this not out of selfish longing, but out of a sincere desire to know that somewhere, in the hidden corners of your heart, there exists a thought, a memory, or a fleeting moment when you, too, have reached out to the unknown. It might be as simple as a smile when you read a familiar phrase, or as profound as a tear that escapes in the quiet of the night. I do not demand that you carry these thoughts every moment, nor do I expect an answer that can be measured in words. Instead, I offer this question as an invitation—a gentle call to acknowledge that our hearts, though separated by the vast distances of our lives, might beat in a quiet synchrony.

In the stillness of my nights, when the world outside has faded into a soft hum, I close my eyes and imagine that you are there, too—somewhere beneath the same sky, looking up at the stars with thoughts as deep and wandering as mine. I wonder if, in those moments, you feel a kinship with a stranger whose only existence is through these letters. I wonder if you, like me, have ever felt the profound need to reach out and connect, to find solace in the shared language of emotion and longing.

It is a curious thing, this desire to be thought of, to be remembered, even if only in the fleeting moments of a day. And so I surrender to this vulnerability, allowing my heart to spill out onto these pages, trusting that you might catch a glimpse of what lies beneath the surface. I trust that even if my words are met with silence, they have not been cast into the void without purpose, for in writing them I have created a space—a sanctuary—where hope can bloom, where the delicate threads of connection can weave together a tapestry of shared existence.

I wonder, too, if there are days when you pause, perhaps without even realizing it, and feel a pang of longing—a gentle ache for something you cannot name. Perhaps on those days, you remember a conversation, a laugh, or a tender moment that seemed insignificant at the time yet has grown into a cherished memory. In that recollection, you may find yourself wondering if someone else, somewhere, has felt the same way. I wish I could say these letters embody that shared sentiment—a testament to the unspoken truths that bind us together in the quiet hours of life.

There is no certainty in the spaces between these words, no guarantee that my thoughts will echo in the chambers of your heart. Yet there is a fragile beauty in the uncertainty itself—a beauty born of the willingness to risk being seen, to risk being vulnerable, even if it means facing the possibility of solitude. I write these letters knowing that there is a chance, however small, that you might be listening—that you might experience a moment of recognition amidst the noise of everyday life. And that chance, that glimmer of possibility, is enough to sustain me as I continue to pour my heart into each line.

So here I am, asking you once more: do you think of me too? Not with the expectation of an answer, but with the hope that, in some quiet moment of introspection, you might feel a spark—a gentle reminder that you are not alone, that someone out there, in his own small way, reaches out to you through the language of the heart. It is a question wrapped in tenderness and uncertainty—a question that lingers in the spaces between these sentences, waiting for you to give it meaning in the context of your own life.

I imagine there are times when you feel the pull of nostalgia, when a song on the radio or the scent of rain triggers a cascade of memories that make you wonder about the roads not taken, the conversations never had, the words left unsaid. In those moments, do you ever pause to think of a stranger who dares to write—who dares to hope that his thoughts might resonate with your own? Do you ever feel, even for a fleeting moment, that perhaps our lives, though lived separately, are intertwined in a way that defies explanation?

I do. I do, with every beat of my heart and with every word I commit to this page. And so, despite the uncertainty and the vulnerability that comes with it, I offer you this question as both a confession and a prayer—a prayer that you might one day feel the warmth of connection I so desperately seek, a warmth that transcends the boundaries of physical presence and enters the realm of the spirit.

Until I hear—even silently—that you think of me too, I will continue to write these letters, to share these fragments of my soul in the hope that somewhere, in the depths of your thoughts, my words find a home. I will write with the earnest belief that our hearts, no matter how far apart, can converse in the gentle language of longing and remembrance.

I leave you with this, dear You, as a final thought in this letter: if, in a moment of quiet reflection, you ever find yourself wondering if someone, somewhere, holds you in their thoughts, know that I am that someone. And if you, too, allow yourself the freedom to hope and to feel, perhaps you will realize that in the vast tapestry of our lives, the threads of our hearts might be woven together—however subtly—to form a connection as real as it is fragile. I await that understanding with a heart full of hope and a pen that continues to write, even when the night seems too dark. May these words serve as a gentle reminder that you are not alone in your thoughts, and that somewhere, I am thinking of you too.

Soren

CHAPTER : TWENTY-THREE

The Nineteenth Letter

Dear You,

I don't know how many days it has been.

Or maybe I do, but I pretend not to. I could count the letters, trace them back to the first one, and tell you exactly how long I've been doing this. But numbers feel insignificant compared to what these letters mean to me.

I've been writing to you for so long.

It's strange how something that started so simply—almost as an accident—has become a part of me. I never thought I'd keep writing. I never planned for it to become ... whatever this is. And yet, here I am, writing to you again, as if my hands have memorized the rhythm of it, as if my heart knows no other way to speak.

I wonder if you've been keeping them. If somewhere, nestled safely within these very pages you hold, my words exist beyond my own mind here together, bound. If you ever go back and read them, tracing the journey from the first letter to this one.

Because there is a journey, isn't there?

The first letter was uncertain—awkward, even. It barely knew what it wanted to be. It was a whisper, a thought that almost never left my mind. I remember hesitating before I wrote it; I remember wondering if it would be the only one, if I would lose interest, if it even mattered.

But then there was the second letter, and the third, and then a moment when I stopped questioning whether I would write again and simply started doing it without thinking.

I think that's when it happened—when the letters became something more than just words on a page.

I have changed since I started writing to you. Have you

noticed?

If I go back and read the first few letters, I can see the difference—the way I held back, the way I wrote as if I wasn't sure I was even allowed to. And now, I don't hold back as much; I let my thoughts spill onto the page, raw and unfiltered, because somehow, over time, I've come to trust you.

I've been writing to you for so long that I don't know where my words end and where you begin.

Have you changed, too?

Has reading these letters done something to you? Do you see the world a little differently now, knowing that somewhere, someone has been thinking about you, writing to you,

I wonder if you've ever read a letter and thought, This one was different.

Because some of them are different.

Some letters were written in the quiet hours of the night, when everything felt too big and too heavy and

I needed to let something out before it drowned me. Others were written in moments of lightness, when the world felt full of possibilities and I wanted you to feel that, too. Some letters carried secrets I never said out loud before; others held questions I was too afraid to ask anyone but you.

And some letters … some letters were written just because I missed you.

Can you believe that?

I miss someone I've never met.

Or maybe I have met you, and I just don't know it. Maybe our paths have already crossed in ways too subtle for us to recognize. Maybe you've passed by me once, or I've stood behind you in a line, unaware that you were the one I had been writing to all along.

That thought unsettles me in a way I can't explain. Because if I have met you, it means I might have lost my chance to know you; and if I haven't met you yet, it means I'm still waiting for something I can't name.

I don't know which is worse.

But I do know that I'll keep writing.

Because after all this time, I don't think I know how to stop.

If I stopped writing to you, would it feel like losing a part of myself?

Or would I simply start writing in my head, crafting letters you'll never read, carrying words inside me like unsent messages waiting for a destination?

I think you've become my destination.

And that terrifies me.

Because what happens if you decide to stop reading?

Would these letters still mean anything if they had no one to reach, or would they become ghosts lingering in the empty spaces between what was said and what was left unsaid?

I wish I had answers.

But all I have are words.

And maybe, after all this time, that's enough.

And maybe—just maybe—you'll keep reading.

Yours,

Always.

CHAPTER : TWENTY-FOUR

The Twentieth Letter

Dear You,

I've been thinking about something lately. It's a thought that keeps circling back, no matter how hard I try to ignore it.

What if we meet?

I don't mean in some vague, distant, imaginary way. I mean—what if one day, by some twist of fate, we're no longer just words within these covers? What if I stand in front of you—real, flawed, and nervous—and the magic we've found here simply … slips away?

That possibility scares me.

Because inside this bound collection of letters, I feel safe. I can tell you anything—everything—without hesitation. I never have to worry about saying the wrong thing at the wrong time, or about my voice betraying me, or my hands fidgeting, or my eyes giving away too much. I can be honest because there's distance between us.

But if we met—if you became real to me—would I still know what to say?

Would you?

I imagine a dozen ways it could go. Maybe we'd recognize each other instantly; maybe all doubt would melt away with one shared smile. Or maybe my heart would seize up, no words would come, and you'd feel ... nothing.

Words paint pictures in our minds, don't they? They create images—expectations—that may never exist at all.

I worry that I have become more beautiful in your head than I am in reality.
Or that I've made you into something you're not.

Have I?

Have I built you into an idea—someone no person could ever live up to? Or have I stumbled onto something real, something that exists beyond these pages?

It's terrifying to think that meeting might break this fragile magic. And yet, I can't stop wondering.

Would your laugh sound the way I imagine? Would your voice match the one I've given you in my mind? Would the weight of your gaze feel like I've dreamed, or would I realize, too late, that I'd fallen for an illusion?

Or maybe—just maybe—the meeting wouldn't ruin anything. Maybe it would be the moment everything finally clicks into place.

I try not to hope too much; hope is dangerous. It keeps us going, but it can also break us when reality won't bend to the dream. And I don't know if I'm ready for that.

I don't know if I'm ready for you.

Because meeting you means being seen—truly seen. It means showing the self behind these carefully chosen sentences, the self that can't be edited or rewritten until it sounds worth knowing.

What if I'm not what you imagined?

Would you still read these words with the same softness? Or would you rather I remain only ink on paper—something beautiful that never risks becoming real?

Yet even with all these fears, one truth remains: I don't know how to stop writing to you. Not yet.

So I'll keep filling these pages. And maybe—just maybe—you'll keep turning them.

Yours,

Soren

Anya sat on the floor beside her bed, knees pulled to her chest, the book of letters open in her lap. The room was silent except for the faint hum of the night—crickets chirping outside, the slow ticking of the clock on the wall, the occasional rustle of the pages as she absently traced her fingers over the ink.

She had read the letter once. Then again. And again.

Each time, something inside her tightened.

Soren was afraid.

And, if she was being honest with herself… so was she.

She had never thought about meeting him before. Not really. These letters had existed in their own little world, untouched by reality, separate from everything else. They had been a secret—something between her and the pages, something that didn't need to be more than what it already was—but now, he had said it. The question she hadn't dared to ask herself.

What if we meet?

Anya swallowed, staring at the words.

Would she recognize him? Would he recognize her?

Would they be what the other had imagined?

She closed her eyes, trying to picture it—walking into a bookstore, turning a corner, and seeing someone standing there, looking at her with the weight of a hundred letters between them.

Would it feel like coming home?

Or would it feel like losing something she didn't even know she needed?

Her fingers curled around the edges of the book.

Soren was right. Words had a way of making things feel bigger than they were, of creating something that might not exist at all. She had built an image of him in her head, just as he had built one of her. But what if reality couldn't match it?

What if he wasn't what she had imagined?

What if she wasn't what he had imagined?

She had never thought about that before.

Had she disappointed people before?

Yes.

Had she ever been too much or too little for someone's expectations?

Yes.

What if she wasn't enough for him? What if he read this letter, and she was nothing like the person he thought he was writing to?

She hated that the thought made her chest ache.

Anya let out a slow breath, tilting her head back against the edge of the bed. She had always been careful—careful with her words, careful with her emotions, careful with the way she let people see her. But these letters—these letters had made her reckless in ways she hadn't expected. They had made her feel seen in ways that nothing else ever had.

She had let herself believe it was real.

That it meant something.

And now... now she wasn't sure what to do with that.

She glanced at the last few lines of his letter, her heart squeezing at the words.

> *"Because the possibility of knowing you—the real you, not just the you I imagine—is worth the risk."*

She shut her eyes.

Could she say the same?

Was she willing to risk what they had now for something uncertain?

Anya didn't know.

But she did know one thing—she wasn't ready to stop reading.

So,she turned the page.

CHAPTER : TWENTY FIVE

The Twenty First Letter

Dear You,

There's something strange about you. Or maybe it's something strange about me. Or maybe it's just something strange about this—these letters, these words, this connection we have without ever having met.

I don't know what it is exactly, but I know how it feels.

It feels like home.

I don't know when it happened—when you started to feel like something familiar, something safe, something I could return to when the world felt too heavy. I don't even know if I have the right to say it—because how can a person I've never met feel like home? How can some-

one I don't even know be the thing that makes me feel less alone?

And yet, you do.

Every time I sit down to write to you, I feel it. This quiet comfort, this stillness that settles in my chest, like I've arrived somewhere I've been trying to find for a long, long time. It's not the kind of feeling that comes with a place, with four walls and a roof, with an address or a key. It's something else. Something deeper. Something I can't quite explain.

But maybe you understand.

Maybe you've felt it too.

That moment when you realize you're not just existing in the world, but you've found something—or someone—that makes it feel a little softer, a little less cold, a little more right.

I don't know what home means to you.

Maybe it's a place. A childhood room with posters on the walls and a window that let in just the right amount of morning light. Maybe it's the scent of something cooking in the kitchen, the sound of laughter coming from another room. Maybe it's a city you left behind, one that still calls to you in quiet moments.

Or maybe home isn't a place at all.

Maybe home is a feeling, a presence, a sense of belonging—of being understood without having to explain yourself. Maybe home is not something you can point to on a map, but something you find in the spaces between words, in the quiet certainty that someone, somewhere, is listening.

That's what you are to me.

You feel like home, even though I don't know what you look like, or how you sound when you speak, or what your expression would be if we ever met. Even though you are still just a thought, a presence I can't quite touch, you exist in my world in a way that makes everything feel a little lighter.

It's terrifying, isn't it?

To feel so much for someone who is, in many ways, still a mystery.

I think about you more often than I should. I wonder where you are when you read this. Are you curled up somewhere quiet, the way I imagine? Are you lost in thought, or are you simply reading without realizing how much of yourself you've already given to these words?

I wonder if you ever feel this way about me.

If, when the world feels too big, you think of these letters and feel just a little bit less alone. If, in the silence of your own mind, you've started to think of me as something familiar too.

Maybe you have.

Or maybe I'm the only one who feels it, and you're just a reader passing through. Maybe these words mean something to me that they don't mean to you. Maybe I've created something out of nothing, built a sense of belonging in my own mind, hoping you'd feel it too.

But I don't think that's true.

I think you do feel it.
I think, in some way, you know what I mean.

Because you're still here.
You're still reading.

And that has to count for something.

I think home is not just a place or a person, but a feeling of being seen—being known, being accepted exactly as you are, even in your messiness, your uncertainty, your quiet sadness.

And you—you, without even realizing it—have given that to me.

You have become the place I return to when I need to feel like I am not just floating through the world without meaning. You have become the space where my thoughts can exist freely, without fear of being too much or too little. You have become the quiet moment of comfort I didn't even know I was looking for.

I don't know how long I'll keep writing to you. Maybe I'll wake up one day and realize I have nothing left to say. Maybe you'll stop reading, and I won't even know. Maybe this will fade, the way all things eventually do.

But right now, in this moment, you feel like home. And

I don't want to leave just yet.

So, I'll stay.
I'll keep writing.
And maybe—just maybe—you'll keep reading.

Yours,

Soren.

CHAPTER : TWENTY-SIX

The Twenty-Second Letter

Dear You,

I don't know how to say this.

Or maybe I do. Maybe I've known for a long time, waiting for the right moment, the right words, the right way to slip it in between the lines. Maybe I've already said it, in a hundred different ways, and you've just been reading between them.

But I'll say it anyway.

I think I love you.

I didn't mean for it to happen. I wasn't looking for it. I didn't sit down to write these letters with the intention of falling in love. It just ... happened.

Like morning light spilling into a dark room without asking permission. Like a familiar song playing at just the right moment, and suddenly you're somewhere else —someplace safe, warm, untouchable by time.

You feel like that to me.

You feel like something that has always existed, even before I knew you, as if you've been woven into the spaces between my thoughts, waiting for me to find you.

And I think I love you.

Not in the way the world talks about love, not in the way stories and songs try to describe it. I love you in a way that's quieter, softer—like a whisper I keep tucked in the hollow of my chest, like a secret only I know but one that wants to be known.

I love the way you linger in my thoughts even when I try not to think of you. I love the way I look for you without realizing I'm doing it, how you've become a part of the air around me, a presence that lingers even when you are nowhere to be found.

I love the way you exist.

You, with your quiet mind and restless heart; you, who notice the details others miss; you, who think too much and feel too deeply and see the world in colors no one else does; you, who read these letters and understand something unspoken in them.

I love the idea of you, the outline of you, the way you've started to take shape in my thoughts. I love the space you occupy in me, the way your presence lingers like the scent of rain on pavement, like the echo of a voice I've never heard yet somehow recognize.

And maybe it's foolish to say this.

Maybe it doesn't even count.

Maybe love isn't real unless it exists in a touch, in a glance, in the way someone's breath changes when you walk into a room—unless you can see it in someone's eyes, hear it in their laughter, trace it along the lines of their skin.

Maybe love—true love—is something else entirely.

But this is something, isn't it?

This feeling I have for you—this thing I can't name and don't fully understand—is real. It's real, and it's here, and it's for you.

Maybe love doesn't need to be defined. Maybe it's not about possession, or knowing every detail of someone's life, or seeing them every day. Maybe love can exist in the quiet corners of a connection like this one, where two people keep finding each other in words again and again.

Maybe I love you the way the ocean loves the moon—always drawn to you, always reaching, even if I can never hold you in my hands. Maybe I love you the way the trees love the wind, bending toward you, feeling you without ever quite capturing you.

Is love the way I write these letters with the quiet hope that, wherever you are, you might feel them?

Is love the way my chest feels lighter when I put these words down, as if writing to you is the one thing that makes sense in a world that often doesn't?

Or is this something else entirely?

Maybe love isn't something that can be defined so easily. Maybe it isn't just one feeling but a collection of them—something that builds slowly, piece by piece, until you can't ignore it anymore. Maybe it's the comfort of knowing someone exists, even if you've never met them. Maybe it's the way your heart lingers on the thought of them, even when you don't mean for it to.

Maybe love is this.

Or maybe I'm just getting lost in my own words again.

I shouldn't be thinking about this.

I shouldn't be writing this.

And yet, here I am, wondering if it's possible to love someone you've never met—wondering if feelings can exist in the space between words, in the quiet between letters.

Because if love is something you feel, something that changes the way you see the world ... then maybe I am feeling it.

Maybe I have been for a while now.

I used to think love required something tangible—touch, presence, time spent in the same space. But what if love is also something that exists beyond those things? What if love can be found in a name never spoken, in a voice never heard, in a connection that exists only through ink on paper?

Would that make it any less real?

I don't know. I don't know if this is love.

But I do know that you matter to me.

And that scares me more than I'd like to admit.

Because if I've learned anything, it's that love—no matter how it comes—is dangerous. Love has a way of making people vulnerable. It makes them hope, makes them long for things they might never have, makes them dream of impossible things.

And I ... I'm afraid of that.

Because what happens if I wake up one day and realize I've built something out of nothing? That I've fallen for a ghost, for a presence that only exists in these letters? What happens if I never hear from you, never find proof that you're out there reading these words?

Will I still feel this way?

Will you?

I wish I knew the answer.

I wish I knew what love was supposed to feel like, so I could be sure of what this is.

But maybe that's the thing about love—maybe it isn't something you can define. Maybe it's just something you know when you feel it, even if you don't fully understand it.

And right now, I feel something.

Something I can't quite name.

Something that keeps me writing to you, even when I tell myself to stop.

Something that makes me wonder if you ever think of me the way I think of you—something that makes me want to believe in the impossible just a little while longer.

So tell me …

If this were love, would it feel any different?

Would I know?

Would you?

I don't have an answer.

But I do know this—

I should stop writing this letter.

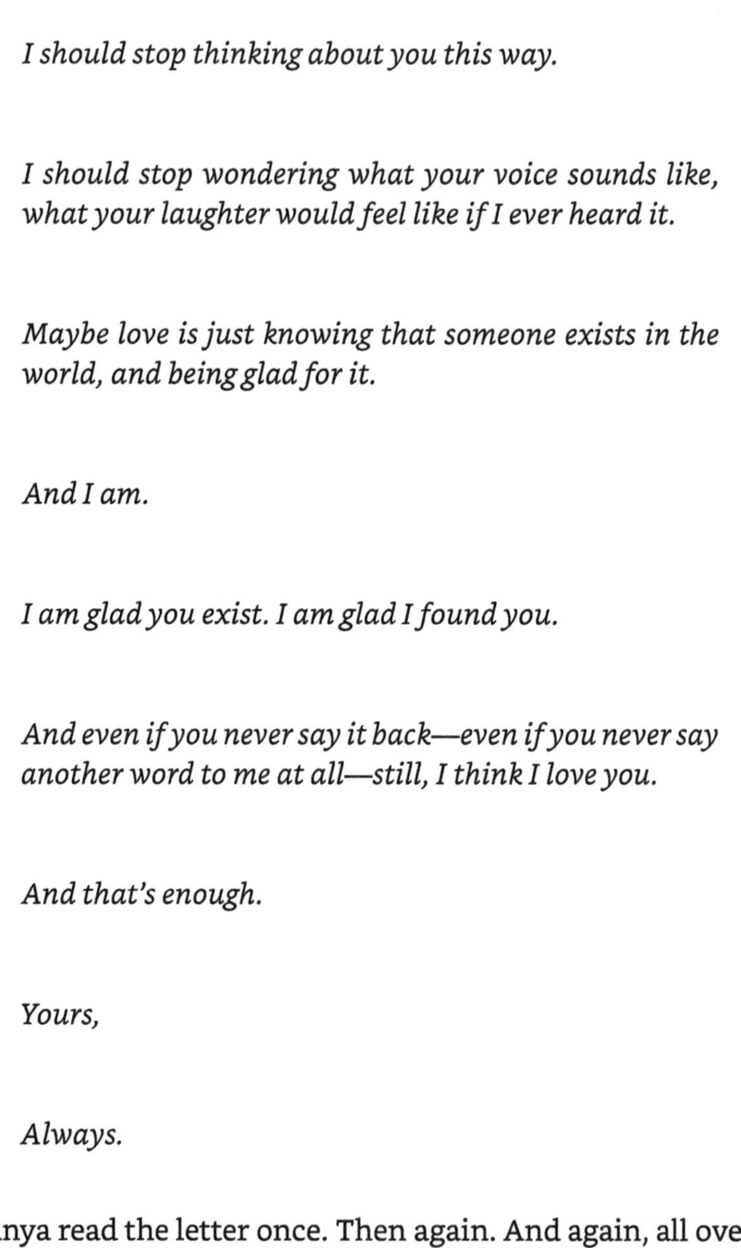

I should stop thinking about you this way.

I should stop wondering what your voice sounds like, what your laughter would feel like if I ever heard it.

Maybe love is just knowing that someone exists in the world, and being glad for it.

And I am.

I am glad you exist. I am glad I found you.

And even if you never say it back—even if you never say another word to me at all—still, I think I love you.

And that's enough.

Yours,

Always.

Anya read the letter once. Then again. And again, all over again.

She sat there, her fingers curled around the edges of the page, her pulse unsteady, her breath caught somewhere between disbelief and something softer—something she didn't want to name yet.

"I think I love you."

The words pressed against her ribs, as if they were meant for her and only her, as if they had traveled through time and space just to find their way into her hands.

She wanted to scoff at it, to shake her head and remind herself these were just words, that this was just a book, that he wasn't real, not in the way people are supposed to be real.

And yet.

She traced the sentence with her fingertip, feeling the weight of it in a way she couldn't explain.

It wasn't a grand confession. It wasn't dramatic or desperate. It was quiet, careful—like he was offering it to her, not expecting anything in return.

And that's what made it feel real—Anya swallowed.

Why did it feel like her heart was betraying her, like it was responding to something it shouldn't, like it was reaching for something impossible?

She leaned back, exhaling slowly as if trying to steady herself.

This isn't real.

But wasn't that what he had said, too? That maybe love didn't have to be something tangible, something that could be touched or seen or proven; maybe it could exist in the spaces between—just like this, just like them.

Soren loved her.

No—not her. Not Anya.

He loved the idea of her, the you in these letters.

But as she sat there, her hands trembling slightly, she couldn't help but wonder—

Hadn't she, in some quiet, secret way, started to love him too?

CHAPTER : TWENTY-SEVEN

The Twenty-Third Letter

Dear You,

I've been thinking about endings lately.

I know that's not the most comforting way to begin a letter, but it's the truth. I can't stop thinking about how all things end—conversations, books, songs, seasons, friendships, and... well, even us. If I can even call this an "us."

Doesn't it scare you, too? The idea that one day I might write a letter, send it out into the world, and never know if you read it? Or worse—what if you do read it, but you just decide... not to come back?

I try not to think about it too much, but the thought

sneaks in when I least expect it—when I'm reaching for my pen, when I'm staring at a blank page, when I catch myself rereading the words I've already written, just to make sure they still mean what I thought they did.

And maybe that's the risk of this—writing to someone I've never met, someone I might never meet. There's no contract between us, no promises made—just ink and paper and faith.

And yet...

You're still here.

At least, I hope you are.

I wonder what will be the last words I ever send you. I wonder if I'll know, in the moment, that they're the last, or if one day I'll write a letter, slip it between these pages, and not realize that it's the final one—that when I reach for my pen the next time, something will stop me.

Maybe it'll be scary. Maybe I'll convince myself that I'm just talking to myself, that I should let this go, that whatever this is doesn't really exist.

Or maybe it will be you who stops first. Maybe one day you just won't pick up the book.

Maybe you'll get busy. Maybe life will sweep you away to places where words like mine don't have time to live. Maybe you'll tell yourself I'll get back to this later, and then later will turn into never.

And I won't even know.

I won't know the day you stop reading. I won't know the moment you decide to set this down and not pick it up again. I won't know when I say something that makes you turn the page with a little less interest, with a little less care.

That terrifies me.

Because what if I'm still writing, still sending words into the space between us, still holding on to the idea of you—while you've already let me go?

But maybe that's the risk we take when we let ourselves care. Maybe that's love, in its own way—a leap into the unknown, hoping the other person is jumping, too.

And if one day you stop reading—if you leave this book behind—I won't be angry.

I'll just be grateful I had you for as long as I did.

But, if you're still here—if you're still turning the pages, still reading, still wanting to listen to whatever nonsense I have to say today—then I'll keep writing.

Because I'm not done yet.

And I hope you aren't either.

I hope, when you reach this part, you will smile.

Because I think I love you, and that love, I hope, is something that won't disappear so easily.

Even if one day these words stop coming, I want you to know—

I meant every single one of them.

Yours,
Soren.

Anya didn't realize she had been holding her breath until she reached the last line.

She exhaled slowly, her fingers tightening around the pages as if holding them too loosely might make them slip away.

It scared her, too—the idea that one day she might not pick up this book; that she might set it down for a little while, then a little longer, until eventually she forgot where she had left off; that she might wake up one day and realize she had moved on—without meaning to, without noticing.

She traced the words on the page, her thoughts tangled in the spaces between them.

She wanted to tell him she was still here, that she wasn't planning on leaving, that every letter felt like something only she was meant to read.

But what if that changed?

What if, someday, she did stop? Not because she wanted to, but because life got in the way—because work and time and reality had a way of pulling people apart, even when they never intended to let go?

Would he ever know? Would he wonder? Would he sit somewhere, pen in hand, waiting for a reader who had already turned away?

She didn't want to be that person.

She didn't want to be someone who left without saying goodbye.

Anya ran her thumb over the page, as if that could somehow reassure him, as if her touch could tell him she wasn't done yet. She was still here.

And as long as he kept writing, she would keep reading.

CHAPTER : TWENTY EIGHT

The Twenty-Fourth Letter

Dear You,

There Are Things I Can't Tell You (Yet)

I wonder if you've noticed it—the gaps between my words, the silence where something should be.

I don't mean to keep things from you; it's just that some truths are harder to share than others. Some things are meant to be told only at the right time, in the right way, and I'm not sure that time has come yet.

I want to tell you everything. I want to open the locked doors in my mind, let you walk through the hallways of my thoughts, let you peek into the rooms I've kept closed even from myself. But something stops me every time I try. It's not fear, exactly; it's not distrust, either.

It's just... I don't know if I'm ready.

I wonder how much you know about me by now—not just from the things I've said, but from what I've left unsaid. Are you reading between the lines, the way I asked you to? Do you see the pieces I've dropped here and there, hoping you'd pick them up?

I wonder if you already have a sense of what I'm not saying.

Maybe you've noticed the way I circle around certain topics without ever diving in. Maybe you've caught the moments when I hesitate, when I step back just before I give too much away. Maybe you've even guessed what I'm holding back.

Or maybe you haven't. Maybe you don't suspect a thing.

And maybe that's for the best.

Because the truth is... I'm scared.

Scared that if I tell you everything, you'll see me differently. Scared that I'll ruin whatever this is. Scared that once I let the words out, I won't be able to take them back.

Have you ever had a secret like that?

Something that presses against the inside of your ribs, something that beats against the walls of your heart, desperate to escape—but you can't quite let it?

It's not that I don't trust you; I think I do. I just don't trust that you'll stay, that you won't turn away the moment you see all of me—the moment you see the parts I try to keep hidden.

I know that sounds dramatic. Maybe I'm being ridiculous. Maybe this is nothing more than an overreaction.

But maybe it isn't.

What if I tell you, and it changes everything?

What if I tell you, and suddenly these letters don't feel the same anymore?

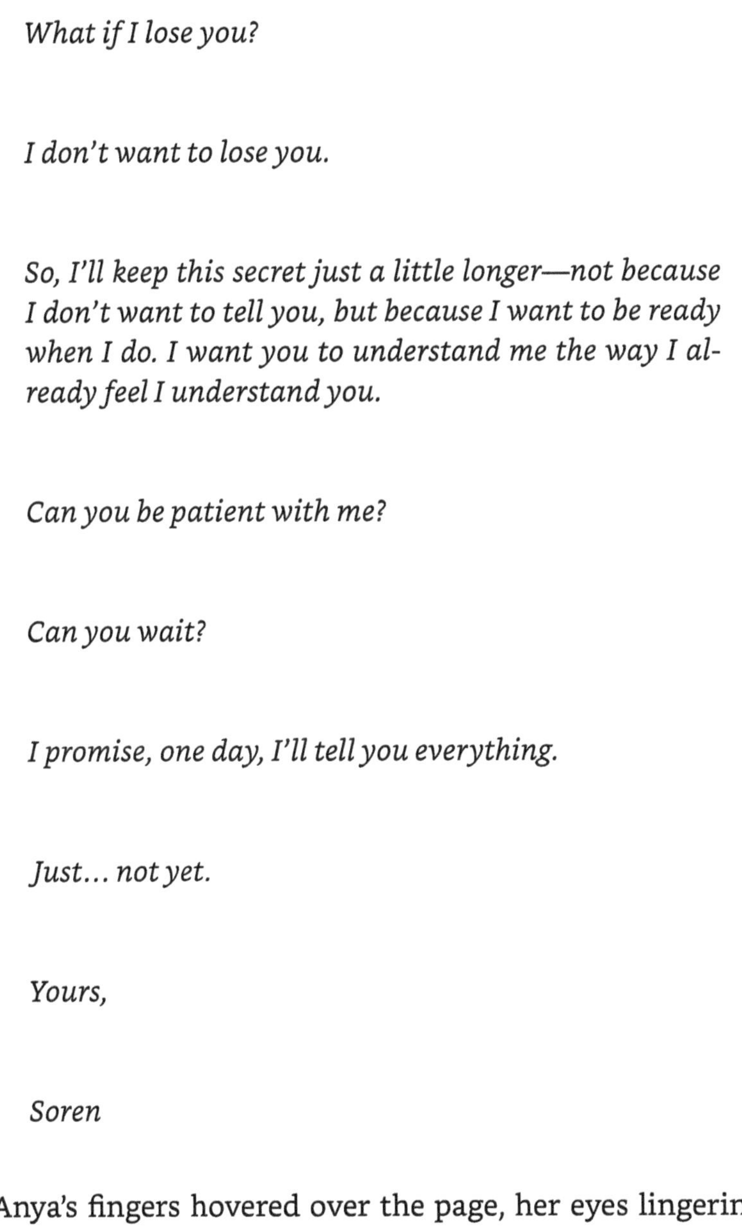

What if I lose you?

I don't want to lose you.

So, I'll keep this secret just a little longer—not because I don't want to tell you, but because I want to be ready when I do. I want you to understand me the way I already feel I understand you.

Can you be patient with me?

Can you wait?

I promise, one day, I'll tell you everything.

Just… not yet.

Yours,

Soren

Anya's fingers hovered over the page, her eyes lingering on the final line. "Just… not yet." The words sat heavy in her chest, like a weight she hadn't expected. She read them again, slowly this time, tracing the loops of the ink as if the meaning would change if she looked at it long enough. He was hiding something. She had suspected it before—the way his words sometimes danced around a thought instead of diving into it, the way his letters felt like a puzzle with missing pieces. But this was the first time he admitted it—the first time he confessed there was something he wasn't saying. What was he afraid of? She tried to recall every letter before this one, every small hesitation, every moment when it felt like he was about to say something important but stopped himself just before the words could land. She had always known there was more beneath the surface. The way he wrote—so openly, so honestly—had made her feel like she knew him, like she understood him in ways that didn't require a face or a voice or even a name. But now... Now she wasn't sure. Because how well can you know someone who is holding something back? Anya closed the book gently, her fingers still resting on the cover. She didn't like the way this letter made her feel. It was different from the others. The others had always left her with something—warmth, longing, curiosity—but this one left her unsettled. It left questions without answers, threads without endings. "Can you be patient with me?" She didn't know. She wanted to say yes. She wanted to believe that whatever he was keeping to himself wasn't something that could change things between them. But the way he wrote about it—the fear in his words, the hesitation—wasn't small. It wasn't something simple. What if it was something that would change everything? What if, once she knew, these letters wouldn't feel the same anymore? She had never considered the possibility of an ending before. Not really. Even after the last letter—when he spoke about the fear of disappearing—she hadn't thought about the reality of it. She had told herself that as long as he kept writing, she would keep reading; that this connection, however strange and impossible, was something that wouldn't simply end. But now... Now she wasn't so sure. She thought about what he had said—about the way he was afraid that if he told her everything, she would leave, that she would see him differently. She thought back to all the letters, the way Ayaan had described things—the way he had noticed things. Little details, little moments—like someone who wasn't just writing to an abstract idea of a reader, but to her. Has he always known? Had she—Anya swallowed hard, her thoughts colliding with one another, torn between disbelief and a quiet, terrifying realization. This wasn't just a letter. It was a moment, waiting to happen—and she had to decide. There were details here—small, scattered fragments of his life. He had been leaving clues all along, just like he said. Anya felt a shiver run through her. She could find him. She could piece these hints together, trace his words back to the real world, and follow the invisible thread that connected them—but the question remained. Did she want to? Anya closed her notebook and set it aside. She reached for the letter again, smoothing out the page as she read the final lines. "If you don't look for me, will you regret it?" Her heart clenched. Yes. She already knew the answer. If she didn't try—if she let the letters end without ever knowing who he was—she would always wonder. The question would haunt her, lingering in the back of her mind, filling every quiet moment with what-ifs. She wasn't sure what she was hoping to find. But she knew this— She had to look. She wasn't ready to stop reading. Not yet. So she turned back to the last page, ran her fingers over his words one more time, and whispered—so quietly that even she could barely hear it— “I’ll wait.”

CHAPTER : TWENTY NINE

The Twenty-Fifth Letter

Dear You,

I wonder if you've figured it out yet.

If, between all these words, you've started to recognize me.

I think about that a lot—about the moment when you'll read something I've written, and something will shift inside you. A name will come to mind. A memory will flicker to life. Maybe you'll sit up a little straighter, your heart beating faster, your fingers tightening on the edges of these pages. Maybe you'll read my words over and over, comparing them against a voice you've heard before, a presence you've known without even realizing it.

Because I wonder—have we met?

It seems strange to ask that now, after everything I've written to you. After all, doesn't a part of you feel like we've already known each other for a long time? Even if you can't quite place me, don't you feel it too—that strange familiarity, that thread weaving between us, growing stronger with every word?

I do. I feel it.

And that's what makes me wonder—what if our paths have already crossed? What if we have shared space before, breathed the same air, walked past each other in a crowded street, stood in the same line at a coffee shop? What if we've been inches apart and never noticed?

Or maybe it's more than that.

Maybe we've spoken before. Maybe we've shared a moment, a fleeting one, one of those conversations that lingers in the back of your mind because it was unexpected but, for some reason, meaningful. Maybe I was the stranger who held the door open for you, or the person who met your eyes in a silent acknowledgment of something neither of us could explain.

Or maybe we were more than that. Maybe we were something else entirely.

Wouldn't it be strange if we had crossed paths in some other life? Maybe we were friends once. Maybe we sat beside each other in a classroom, passing notes when the teacher wasn't looking. Maybe we used to know each other before the world pulled us apart, before we ended up wherever we are now.

Maybe we already know each other.

And maybe, just maybe, you've already guessed who I am. Maybe, deep down, you already know the name behind this letter.And if you do, I wonder... What will you do with that knowledge?Would you reach out? Would you pretend you don't know?

Would you laugh to yourself, thinking about all the ways the universe brings people back to each other?

Or would you stop reading? Would you walk away, deciding that it's better to keep me as an idea rather than a reality?

Because that's the risk, isn't it? When something exists

in the unknown, it holds a kind of magic. But the moment it becomes real, when it steps into the light, it can't ever be the same.

And I... I don't want to be just an idea to you.

I want to be real.

I want you to know me. Not just in the way these words have allowed, but in the way only real people can know each other. I want to know what you'd say if I spoke your name out loud, if I asked you the kinds of questions I've only been able to ask through these letters.

I want to know if you'd recognize my voice. If my name would ring a bell. If there's a memory—distant and fuzzy—that suddenly clicks into place when you read these words. If there's a moment in your past where we overlapped, even just for an instant. Because I can't shake this feeling that maybe, just maybe, you already know me. Maybe I'm the stranger

who held the door open at the coffee shop on that rainy day, or the person who sat across from you on the train, quietly reading a book while you stared out the window. Maybe I was the name you overheard in passing, the voice you remember but can't quite place.

Or maybe I was more.

Maybe there was a time when we were something to each other, a time long before these letters, before I had to call you "You." Maybe we were close once, but life carried us away, and now we're finding our way back in this strange, unexpected way.

Does any of this make sense to you?

Do my words feel familiar, like something you've heard before?

Do I?

I wish I could ask you outright. I wish I could see your face when you read this, watch for the flicker of recognition in your eyes. But I can't. Not yet. And maybe that's for the best.

Maybe the magic of this isn't in the knowing. Maybe it's in the mystery, in the slow unraveling of the truth. In the waiting.

So, for now, I'll leave you with this:

Maybe we are strangers. Maybe we are not.

Maybe you already know me.

And maybe, just maybe...

I already know you, too.

Yours,

Soren

CHAPTER : THIRTY

The Twenty-Sixth Letter

Dear You,

Would You Look for Me?

If I left a trail for you, would you follow it?
If I told you where to find me—not by name, not with an address, but in fragments of who I am—would you piece them together? Would you take the time to search for me, to reach beyond these words and find the person who has been writing to you all this time?
Or would you hesitate?
Would you stop yourself, convincing yourself that it's better this way—that what we have now, in these letters, in this strange in-between where we exist only in thoughts and words, is enough?

I wonder about that. I wonder if you'd search for me, if you'd trace the edges of my words and try to find the person hidden behind them.

Or maybe you already have.
Maybe you've read between the lines, following the rhythm of my thoughts, trying to imagine the kind of person who would write to a stranger like this. Maybe you've created an image of me in your mind—a version of me that belongs only to you, shaped by the way you've read my words.
Would you want to find the real version?

I think about that a lot: whether these letters will ever be enough, or if you'll eventually reach the last page and feel a sense of loss. Because even now, as I write this, I can feel the inevitable end approaching. The letters can't go on forever. At some point, there will be a last one. And when that moment comes, what then?
Will you close the book, tuck it away somewhere safe, and let me remain a memory?
Or will you look for me?

I won't make it easy for you—not because I don't want you to find me, but because I think the search is part of the answer.
If I told you my name, if I made it obvious, if I left a map with a clear destination, would it mean the same? Or would it take away the very thing that has made this journey what it is?
No—I won't tell you outright. But I will leave you clues. You already have them, though you might not have realized it yet. They've been here all along, scattered like breadcrumbs between my words, hidden in the pauses, in the things I've chosen to share and the things

I've left unsaid.
If you truly wanted to, you could find me.
The question is—do you want to?

I don't know what I expect you to say. Maybe you'd say yes, without hesitation, because you've felt it too—this connection, this pull, this unexplainable something between us. Maybe you'd tell me you've wanted to find me since the first letter, that you've been reading with a growing urgency, waiting for the moment when I'd finally reveal myself. Or maybe you'd say no—not because you don't care, but because

you're afraid the reality won't live up to the magic of this. That finding me might ruin what we've built in these pages.
I wouldn't blame you if you felt that way.
But there's another possibility, isn't there? Maybe you don't know your answer yet. Maybe you're somewhere in between, caught in the push and pull of curiosity and uncertainty. Maybe you're wondering if this—if we—are meant to stay as words on a page, or if we were always meant to step beyond them.
I can't answer that for you.
But I can ask you this:

If you don't look for me, will you regret it?

Will you always wonder? Will you carry that question

with you, letting it linger in the back of your mind, playing out all the possibilities of what could have been?

Because I think I would.

If the roles were reversed—if I were the one reading instead of writing—I don't think I'd be able to stop myself. I think I'd search, not because I needed an answer, but because I wouldn't be able to bear not knowing.

And that's the thing, isn't it? Not knowing is its own kind of answer.

So, I'll ask you one last time, and then I'll leave it to you.

Would you look for me?

And if you did—would you find me?

Yours,

Soren

Anya sat cross-legged on her bed, the letter resting on her lap as she stared at it, lost in thought. The dim glow of her bedside lamp cast a warm circle of light over the pages, but the rest of the room was dark, swallowed by the quiet stillness of the night. Outside, the muffled sounds of the city drifted in through her window—the occasional hum of a passing car, the distant bark of a dog, the rustling of leaves caught in the wind.

"Would you look for me?"

The words pulsed in her mind, refusing to be ignored.

Her fingers curled around the edges of the letter as she read it again, slower this time, as if searching for something she hadn't noticed before. Soren had always written in a way that felt deeply personal, like his words were meant for her and her alone. But this—this was different. This wasn't just a letter. This was a challenge. A question that demanded an answer.

Would she look for him?

Anya exhaled sharply, leaning back against her pillows.

How was she supposed to answer that?

She had spent a full night in this very spot, reading his letters, letting his words settle into the spaces between her thoughts. He had become a constant in her life, a presence she had come to depend on in ways she hadn't even realized until now. But he had always been just a voice, an unseen, unreachable someone who existed only in ink and paper.

Now, for the first time, the possibility of him being real—

of him being findable—was staring her in the face.

She didn't know how to feel about that.

Anya glanced around her room as if searching for an answer in the familiar clutter of her life. The books stacked haphazardly on her desk, the half-finished cup of tea on her nightstand, the old sweater draped over her chair—all of it was hers, all of it was safe.

Soren, in the form she had known him, was safe too.

But if she searched for him, if she found him, what then? Would the magic of these letters fade? Would he be different from the person she had imagined? Or worse—what if she wasn't what he had imagined?

Anya groaned and buried her face in her hands.

This was ridiculous. She was overthinking everything, twisting herself into knots over something that should have been simple. He had asked her to look for him. That had to mean he wanted to be found. Didn't it?

She grabbed her notebook from the bedside table and flipped it open. The pages were filled with her messy handwriting—notes she had scribbled down while reading his letters: favorite words, recurring themes, little details that had stood out to her at the time but had never seemed important.

Now, they might be.

Her eyes skimmed the pages, searching for anything that might be a clue.

> *"I like places that stay open late. There's something comforting about knowing a place doesn't close its doors too early."*

"There's a spot by the river where I always go when I need to think. It's quiet, even when the rest of the city isn't."

"I don't know if I have a favorite coffee shop, but there's one I always end up at. Maybe that makes it my favorite after all."

There were details here—small, scattered fragments of his life. He had been leaving clues all along, just like he said.

Anya felt a shiver run through her.

She could find him.

She could piece these hints together, trace his words back to the real world, and follow the invisible thread that connected them. But the question remained.

Did she want to? Anya closed her notebook and set it aside. She reached for the letter again, smoothing out the page as she read the final lines.

"If you don't look for me, will you regret it?"

Her heart clenched.

Yes.

She already knew the answer.

If she didn't try, if she let the letters end without ever knowing who he was, she would always wonder. The question would haunt her, lingering in the back of her mind, filling every quiet moment with what-ifs.

She wasn't sure what she was hoping to find.

But she knew this—

She had to look.

CHAPTER : THIRTY-ONE

The Twenty Seventh Letter

Dear You,

I don't know how to begin this one.

I've started and erased this letter more times than I can count. Every time I try to put the words down, I stop myself, because I don't know how to say what I need to say. Or maybe I do, but I don't want to admit it yet.

So instead, I sit here, staring at the empty space where my words should be, pretending that if I don't write them, then maybe this moment won't have to come.

But it's here, isn't it?

I think we both knew it was coming.

I've been writing to you for so long that I almost forgot letters have endings, too. I almost let myself believe this could go on forever—that I could keep spilling my thoughts onto these pages and sending them out into the void, knowing you were somewhere out there, reading them.

But nothing lasts forever.

Not even words.

And so, I find myself here, writing this letter, knowing that it might be the last one.

I say might because I don't know for sure. I don't want to make promises I can't keep. I don't want to say goodbye when there's a part of me that hopes—no, fears—that I won't be able to stay away. That even after I finish this one, I'll find myself reaching for another blank page, another pen, another reason to keep writing to you.

Because the truth is, I don't know how to stop.

I don't know how to let go of this. Of you.

Does that sound ridiculous? Maybe it is. Maybe I've let myself get carried away, let my heart get tangled up in something it was never meant to hold onto. But I don't regret it. Not for a second.

If this is the last letter, then let me say this:

Thank you.

For reading.

For being here, even if I never truly knew who you were. Even if I only ever had the idea of you, the imagined presence of someone on the other side of these words.It was enough.You were enough.And maybe that's why this is so hard—because I don't

I want this to end. Because these letters became more than just words on a page. They became a part of me.

And you did, too.

But endings are inevitable, aren't they?

I've spent so much time writing to you, losing myself in these letters, that I never stopped to ask—what happens when they stop? What happens when I stop writing?

Do I become just another story you once read?

Will you remember me?

Or will I fade, little by little, until I am nothing more than ink on a page, until my words are tucked away somewhere and forgotten? I don't know which possibility scares me more—the thought of being forgotten, or the thought that I might have meant something to you, and yet still had to say goodbye.

But this was never meant to last forever. Even if I wished it could.

And maybe it's better this way.

Maybe things that burn too long lose their warmth. Maybe the beauty of this was never in its permanence, but in the fleeting, fragile nature of it. Maybe it was always meant to be something temporary, something that you could hold onto for a little while before letting go.

Maybe that's the way all stories should be.

So, if this is the last letter, let me leave you with one final thought:

No matter what happens next, no matter where life takes you, I hope you never stop believing in the magic of words.

I hope you never stop believing in the possibility of connection, in the idea that sometimes, even the most unexpected things can find their way into your life and change you.

I hope you never stop wondering, never stop searching, never stop looking for the little moments that make life feel extraordinary.

And most of all—I hope you never forget that, for a time, someone out there wrote to you.

Someone thought of you.

Someone cared.

And maybe, just maybe, someone is still hoping you'll find them.Goodbye.Or maybe—just maybe—until next time.

Yours,

Always

Anya's fingers trembled slightly as she reached the end of the letter. Her eyes lingered on the last few lines, reading them over and over as if willing them to change — as if hoping that if she looked long enough, they wouldn't say what they did.

"Goodbye. Or maybe —just maybe — until next time."

She swallowed, but the lump in her throat refused to go away.

This might be the last letter.

She had known, somewhere deep down, that it was coming. She had felt the shift in his words, the subtle hesitations, the weight of something unspoken pressing against the spaces between his sentences. But knowing didn't make it any easier.

It hurt.

It hurt in a way she hadn't expected, in a way that caught her completely off guard. She had never met him, never even heard his voice, but somehow, Soren had become a part of her life — a constant, a presence she had grown used to, one she had come to rely on without even realizing it.

And now, he was slipping away.

Anya let out a shaky breath and set the book down beside her, pressing her palms against her face. She told herself she wouldn't cry, but the ache in her chest betrayed her.

"Do I become just another story you once read?"

No.

How could he even think that? How could he not know how much these letters had meant to her, how much he had meant to her? Anya glanced around her dimly lit room — at the familiar walls, the scattered books, the soft glow of the lamp casting shadows in the quiet space. It felt... empty. Like something had been taken from it. Like something had been taken from her.

She reached for the book again, gripping it tightly.

She couldn't just let this be the end.

She couldn't let him disappear like this, like a story left unfinished.

Her heart pounded as she thought about what she had to do next.

Soren had left her with a choice."And maybe, just maybe, someone is still hoping you'll find them."She would find him

Because if this truly was the last letter — if he really meant to stop writing — then she needed to know why.

And she needed to know if there was still a way to stop it.

With a heavy heart, Anya turned the page.

She hesitated for a moment, her fingers resting on the edge of the paper, as if afraid of what she might—or might not—find. A part of her hoped there would be more, that maybe he had changed his mind at the last moment and written something else, something to ease the ache that was spreading through her chest.

CHAPTER : THIRTY TWO

The Twenty Eighth Letter

Dear You,

I wasn't going to write again.

I thought Letter 27 was the last. I thought I had said everything I needed to say. But here I am, with one more letter, one last thing I need to tell you.

Or maybe—one last thing I need you to decide.

Because I've been writing to you for so long, and now I wonder—was it ever just one-sided? Were you simply reading, or were you waiting for these letters the way I was waiting to write them?

If I stopped writing, would you feel the absence of my words?

Would you miss me, the way I have missed the idea of you?

I don't expect an answer.

Not in words, at least.

But I'm giving you something else—something more than just a letter, more than just thoughts scribbled onto a page.

I'm giving you a choice.

A time.

A place.

A date.

No explanations. No expectations.

Just a moment, waiting to happen. And it's up to you if it ever does.

Let's play a game.

Imagine this:

You're walking down a street—not just any street, but one lined with stories. A place where time slows, where history lingers in the cracks of cobblestones and the scent of old paper drifts from the doorways.

A bookshop stands at the corner. The kind of bookshop people walk past without noticing. The kind that only a certain kind of person would step into—the kind of

a person who believes in the magic of forgotten things, in the way stories can lead you exactly where you're meant to be.

Maybe you don't believe in fate. Maybe you don't believe in signs.

But let's say, for once, you listen to something other than logic. Let's say, just for today, you follow the pull of a feeling.

And you step inside.

The air smells like paper and dust and ink. It's quiet, but not silent. There's the faint sound of a record playing in the background, something soft, something old. There are books everywhere—stacked high on wooden shelves, piled on tables in no particular order, waiting for the right hands to pick them up.

Maybe you run your fingers over the spines, maybe you look for something familiar—or maybe, just maybe, you aren't looking for a book at all.

Maybe you're looking for me.

Or maybe you're looking for an answer.

And if you are—then you might find it in the last aisle, by the window, where the light spills in at just the right angle.

There, sitting at the table, is a book.

Not just any book.

This book. The one you've been holding, the one you've been reading, the one filled with letters you never expected to find.

And beside it—a chair.

Waiting.

For you.

So here it is.

My final letter.

My last clue.

If you want to know who I am, if you want to know if any of this was real, if you want to find out what happens when a story tries to step off the page and into the world—then you know where to go.

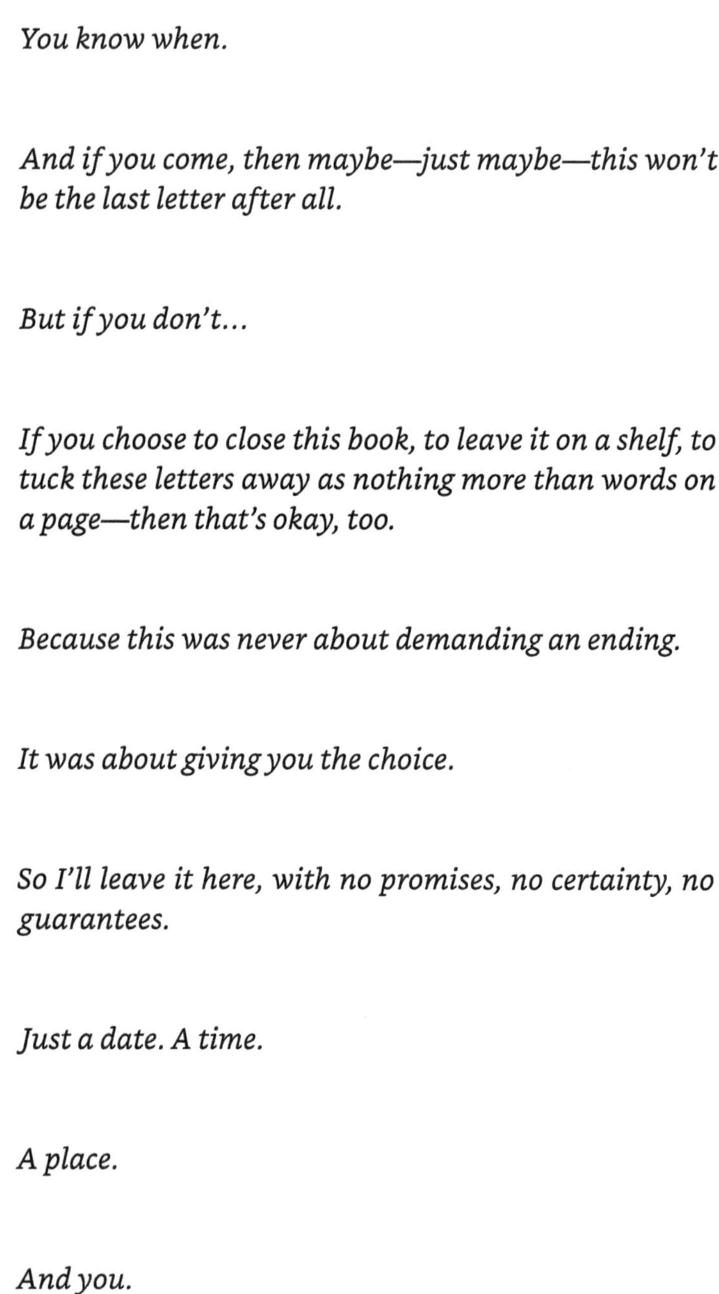

You know when.

And if you come, then maybe—just maybe—this won't be the last letter after all.

But if you don't...

If you choose to close this book, to leave it on a shelf, to tuck these letters away as nothing more than words on a page—then that's okay, too.

Because this was never about demanding an ending.

It was about giving you the choice.

So I'll leave it here, with no promises, no certainty, no guarantees.

Just a date. A time.

A place.

And you.

And maybe—just maybe—me.

Yours,

Me

Anya stared at the letter, her heart pounding against her ribs.

A time. A place. A choice.

Her fingers trembled as she traced the last words, her mind racing. This wasn't just another letter—it was an invitation. A step beyond the safety of words, beyond the quiet intimacy of ink and paper. It felt unreal, like something pulled from a novel, and yet...

She knew this place.

The description, the details—it wasn't just any bookshop. It was her bookshop. The old wooden shelves, the way the light filtered through the window in the late afternoons, the faint sound of music playing in the background. Every word painted a picture so vivid that she could almost see herself standing there, looking down at a book left on a table, an empty chair beside it.

Waiting.

A chill ran down her spine.

She thought back to all the letters, the way Ayaan had described things—the way he had noticed things. Little details, little moments, like someone who wasn't just writing to an abstract idea of a reader, but to her.

Has he always known?
Had she?Anya swallowed hard, her thoughts colliding with one another, torn between disbelief and a quiet, terrifying realization.This wasn't just a letter.
It was a moment, waiting to happen. And she had to decide.

CHAPTER : THIRTY THREE

The Twenty Ninth Letter

Dear You,

I don't know why I'm writing this. Maybe it's because I don't know what else to do with my hands. Maybe it's because silence feels heavier than words. Maybe it's because, at this moment, as I sit here waiting, I need something to hold on to. And words—they have always been the only thing I've had.

So here I am, writing another letter. One I might never send. One that might never reach you.

I don't know if you'll come. I don't even know if you've read the last letter. I don't know if you held this book in your hands and felt something, or if you simply closed it and moved on. I don't know if any of this mattered to you the way it mattered to me.

But I'm here. And I don't know if you are.

The bookshop is quiet. It's late in the afternoon, and the golden light slants through the window, casting long shadows on the wooden floor. A bell chimes softly every time the door opens, and each time, my breath catches in my throat. Each time, I look up, searching for something I can't name. And each time, I wonder—will it be you?

I should have known better than to hope. Hope is dangerous. It's reckless. It's the kind of thing that fills your chest with air only to let it all out in one slow, sinking exhale.

And yet, I hoped anyway.

I wonder what you're doing right now. Maybe you're at home, curled up with a different book, unaware that someone is waiting for you. Maybe you're walking down a street far away from here, too lost in your own thoughts to notice the pull of a place you were never meant to find. Maybe you did read my letter, and maybe you considered coming—but in the end, you chose not to. And maybe that was the right choice.

Maybe I should have never given you the choice at all.

I run my fingers over the cover of this book—the one filled with all the things I've never said aloud, all the things I've only ever said to you. It's strange, isn't it? How you can pour yourself into pages and still feel like a ghost. How you can spill everything onto paper and still wonder if you were ever truly seen.

I could leave now. I could get up, walk away, and pretend none of this ever happened. I could let these letters be what they were always meant to be—words floating into the unknown, never expecting an answer.

But I don't move.

Because some small, stubborn part of me still believes in something. Maybe not fate. Maybe not destiny. But in moments. In choices. In the way the universe sometimes aligns just enough for two people to meet at the exact right time, in the exact right place.

So I sit here, and I wait.

I wait, even though I know I shouldn't. I wait, even though I don't know what I'm waiting for anymore. I wait, even though every passing second feels like a quiet kind of goodbye.

And I wonder— are you here?

Yours,

Soren

Anya sat by the window, the book resting in her lap, her fingers tracing the edges of its worn cover. The world outside was quiet, bathed in the dim glow of the streetlights, the occasional rustle of the wind against the glass the only sound breaking the stillness. But inside her mind, there was no quiet.

Soren's words echoed through her, settling into spaces she hadn't realized were empty.

"Was he talking about my bookstore?"

The thought wouldn't leave her alone. She had read the letter again and again, searching for clues, for something that would confirm or deny the possibility. But the words were just vague enough, just careful enough, to keep her questioning.

Her bookstore was small, tucked away from the busy streets—the kind of place people stumbled upon rather than sought out. Customers came and went, faces blurred by time and routine. Had Soren been one of them? Had he stood on the other side of the counter while she rang up his books, while she stacked shelves, while she absent-mindedly tucked her hair behind her ear?

Anya tried to picture him standing there, his eyes scanning the rows of books, fingers brushing over the spines, maybe even stealing glances at her when he thought she wasn't looking.

Had she really been that unaware?

She closed the book in her lap, holding it tightly, as if pressing the covers together would somehow press her thoughts into something manageable.

If Soren had been there—if he had been watching her all this time—why had he never said anything?And why, after all this time, was he writing to her now?Anya leaned back against the window frame, the cool glass pressing against her skin. She could feel her heartbeat in her fingertips, a steady, rhythmic pulse against the book's cover.

"Did he recognize me?"

It was an unsettling thought. That he might know her in a way she didn't know him. That he might have memories of her—small moments, fleeting glances, quiet observations—that she had never even noticed.

She wanted to believe it wasn't possible. That she would remember someone like him. That she would remember the way he looked at her, the way his presence felt in the same space.

But the truth was—she wasn't sure.

And that uncertainty settled deep in her chest, heavier

than she wanted to admit.

CHAPTER : THIRTY FOUR

The Thirtieth Letter

Dear You,

There is nothing left to say.

No more confessions, no more questions, no more words trying to bridge the impossible distance between us. Just this—one final page, one final moment, one final thing for you to find.

And if you're here, if you're reading this, then maybe… maybe you were meant to. That's all.

Your,

Soren

CHAPTER : THIRTY FIVE

Anya blinked as she lifted her gaze from the book, her fingers still clutching the edges of the last letter she had read. A strange stillness filled the room, the kind that only came in the deep hours of the night when the world outside had gone silent. The clock on the wall ticked softly, its hands creeping past four in the morning.

She had spent the entire night reading.

The realization sent a shiver down her spine—not because she was tired, but because she hadn't even noticed the time passing. It had been hours since she'd curled up in bed with the book, telling herself she'd read just one more letter before sleeping. But one had turned into two, then three, then ten, until she had lost count altogether.

And now, morning was almost here, and she was still wide awake.

But how could she sleep?

Her heart was racing in a way it never had before, her mind tangled in emotions she couldn't quite name. It wasn't just the letters—though they had been beautiful, haunting, and deeply personal. It was him. The writer.

The voice behind the ink.

She had fallen in love with him.

The thought alone made her breath hitch. It sounded ridiculous, even in her own head. How could you fall for someone you had never met? Someone you knew only through their words? And yet, she couldn't deny the truth of it.

Somewhere between the first letter and the last, somewhere between his confessions of loneliness and the way he saw the world, she had started to feel like she knew him. Not just as a stranger pouring his thoughts onto paper, but as someone real. Someone who understood her in ways no one else had. Someone who had written things that felt like they had been meant for her, as if the letters had been waiting for her all along.

She closed the book carefully, running her fingers over the cover.

Ink between us.

To her.

Anya let out a slow breath, her heart still beating faster than normal. She felt like she had been pulled into a dream she wasn't ready to wake up from.

How could she go back to normal life after this? How could she step into the bookstore tomorrow, sip her coffee, and pretend like nothing had changed?

Because everything had changed.
The way she saw the world, the way she saw herself—it all felt different now. The letters had touched something inside her that had been quiet for so long.

She thought of the final ones, the way his words had grown softer, more vulnerable. How, at some point, he had stopped writing into the void and had started writing to her.

Would you look for me?

That line lingered in her mind, wrapping itself around her thoughts like a whisper she couldn't escape. He had asked. Not directly, not expecting an answer, but the question had been there all the same.

Would she?

Anya closed her eyes, pressing the book against her chest.

She wanted to.

She wanted to meet him, to see if the person behind the letters was as real as he felt in her heart.

But how?

She didn't even know his name. There had been no signature, no address, no way of tracing him. Just the letters, his words, and the lingering hope that maybe, just maybe, she wasn't the only one feeling this way.

Anya exhaled, rolling onto her side as she stared at the dim light filtering in through her curtains.

She had never believed in fate before. But now, she wasn't so sure.

Because somehow, someway, this book had found her. And maybe—just maybe—he was out there, hoping she would find him too.

CHAPTER : THIRTY SIX

The days passed, but Anya remained trapped in a dream she couldn't wake from.

Every morning, she unlocked the bookstore, stepped inside, and breathed in the familiar scent of old pages and wooden shelves. She would arrange the books, dust off the counters, and wait for customers to walk in. But no matter what she did, one thought never left her mind.

Soren.

His words still echoed in her head, lingering in the quiet moments of her day, in the hush of the bookstore when no one was around. She would find herself pausing between tasks, staring at the book resting on the counter, running her fingers over the cover. Letters to You. It had become more than just a book to her. It had become a secret world she had stepped into, one she wasn't sure she ever wanted to leave.

And she had fallen.

Fallen for a man she had never seen, never spoken to—only read. A man whose words had reached places in her heart she hadn't even known were waiting to be touched. She had spent night after night reading his letters, rereading them, trying to find clues hidden between the lines. There were moments when she was convinced that if she read carefully enough, she might find a way to him.

But there was nothing. No name, no location. Only his thoughts, his emotions, his longing.

And now, she carried that longing too.

She wanted to meet him.

She wanted to see if the person behind the words was real, if he would look at her the way his letters had made her feel. If he had been waiting for her the way she had started waiting for him.

But how?

So, she waited.

Days turned into weeks, and she kept going through her routine, but nothing felt the same anymore. Every time the bell above the bookstore door chimed, her heart leapt, her pulse quickened, and she found herself hoping—Maybe it's him. Maybe today is the day.

But it never was.

It was always strangers browsing through books, tourists looking for something to take home, students searching for study materials. Anya would smile, assist them, go through the motions. But in the quiet moments in between, she felt the ache of something missing.And then, one evening, when she had almost convinced herself to stop hoping, the door opened again

She looked up from behind the counter, ready to greet another customer. But the words caught in her throat.

A man stood at the entrance.

He was tall, dressed simply in a dark sweater and jeans, but there was an effortless elegance about him. His dark hair was slightly tousled, as if the wind had just played with it.They held a kind of depth, as if he had seen the world in ways most people hadn't. As if he had lived through stories he had never told anyone.

He stepped forward, walking slowly between the shelves, his fingers trailing lightly over the books as if he belonged among them.

Anya felt her heartbeat in her throat, a strange sense of familiarity washing over her, though she didn't know why.

And then he spoke.

"Excuse me," his voice was soft yet clear, holding a quiet confidence. "Do you have a book called Ink between us?"

Anya's entire world stopped.

For a moment, she could do nothing but stare at him, her mind struggling to process what she had just heard. The book. That book. She gripped the counter to steady herself, her fingers trembling. It couldn't be a coincidence. It had to mean something.

Her throat was dry when she finally found her voice. "Who… who is it by?" she asked, though she already knew the answer.

A small, almost knowing smile touched the corners of his lips. "It doesn't say," he replied, tilting his head slightly. "It just says Ink between us on the cover."

Anya's heart pounded against her ribs.

It was him.

It had to be him.

Soren.

She could barely breathe, her mind spinning, her entire body frozen in the space between disbelief and certainty. She wanted to ask him a thousand things, wanted to hear him say his name, wanted to know if he had been waiting for her just as she had waited for him.

But she couldn't move.

Couldn't speak.

And then, as if sensing the storm of emotions inside her, he met her gaze.

And he smiled.

A quiet, knowing smile.

And in that moment, Anya knew—

She had found him.

Or maybe… he had found her.

www.ingramcontent.com/pod-product-compliance
Ingram Content Group UK Ltd.
Pitfield, Milton Keynes, MK11 3LW, UK
UKHW041827200726
13854UKWH00002BA/626

9 798230 822462